THE RIVER'S TALE

THE HUDSON GORGE

Photo by Carl Heilman II

THE
RIVER'S
TALE

A NOVEL

BY MICHAEL VIRTANEN

LOST POND PRESS, SARANAC LAKE, NY

For Alexandra

Published by Lost Pond Press,
Saranac Lake, NY 12983.
www.LostPondPress.com

ISBN: 978-0-9789254-4-4

This is a work of fiction.
The extraordinary places are there.
The characters, while inspired by extraordinary
people in those places, are not.

Cover & frontispiece photos by Carl Heilman II
www.carlheilman.com

Back-cover photo by Susan Bibeau

Book design by Susan Bibeau

Copy editing by Akum Norder

Printed by Versa Press, East Peoria, IL

Acknowledgments

Several people read and improved the early manuscript drafts and kept this thing going. I'm grateful to Valerie Bauman, Ben Dobbin, Jeff Foley, Ali Havener, Terry Kassof, Matt Smith, and Pam Walsh. And especially to the writer Steve North for structural clarity, to Dr. Pamela Thacher for language I didn't know, to friend, editor, and publisher Phil Brown for adventures and really old philosophers, and to Saundra, who wrote the first sentence and patiently brought it all home. I will be forever indebted to the Adirondack river guide known to some as God's Flower. Nothing has been the same since.

You can't step into the same river twice.

—HERACLITUS

I

As Alison Reade packed her bags, she clenched her jaw and swallowed the panic rising in her throat. She made an effort to turn off her mind, to slow the runaway freight train of terrifying thoughts. She realized she was tired. The thing right now was to keep moving. And not think. She threw all her clothes into a duffel bag and hard suitcase and left just about everything else behind—her teapot, cereal bowl, smattering of plates. Her aunt would have enough housewares anyway. The only thing she wanted was out, immediately. She even left her textbooks. Classes were done, and she'd only get a couple dollars for the heavily annotated texts, the margins covered in her precise script. Forget her observations about cognitive dissonance. There were no more contradictions.

Will wasn't her lover anymore, not her man, not even her ex. He wasn't the guy she missed sometimes, wondering if she should reconsider him and his professed devotion. No longer was she questioning the breakup night as an aberration, a one-time thing. Now he was just a stalker. That was the last 3 a.m. phone call he'd ever make to her. She hated him now. To be more precise, she was frightened of him, something that had never happened before with men, not walking home alone late one spring night after clubbing, past the dealers and hustlers, who made her laugh with their taunts and come-ons, not even after working part time in the psych ward when one truly dangerous former inpatient called her at home to talk about his gun, his rage, and his thoughts of suicide.

Instead of going to her mother's house, back on Long Island where she had met Will, she was leaving again. Done with the third-floor apartment in the city, where he'd sat in his pickup truck across the street, outside the Korean grocery, until she pointed him out to the two cops who just happened to be parked nearby. He had followed her car all the way from Huntington, pounding on her window at a stoplight and then nearly running her off the road. The cops, sitting in their patrol car, at first disbelieved her when she walked up and asked: What do you do when somebody's chasing you? They thought she was joking. She had composed herself to ask the question. Then she burst into tears and pointed out Will, who was sitting in his truck down the street. The plump black cop got out and started walking toward the pickup and yelled, "Hey." Will drove off like it wasn't about him. They didn't pursue him. That was two weeks ago.

Then the phone calls came. He somehow got her number even though it was listed to somebody else. But Alison focused, with the same cool demeanor she learned she had after Jennie O'Toole threatened her and beat her up in junior-high school, at the end of a long bus ride toward home. Alison told nobody and went back to school the next day and acted like nothing happened.

This time, with the same determination, she wrote her last papers and took the remaining final to finish the master's degree. The Reades hold their heads up. That's what her mother said. And she hated the prissy patrician sound of it. But now, instead of continuing on for the Ph.D. and the position as a teaching assistant and a part-time job in the counseling center for troubled undergraduates, instead of the free tuition and small stipend, she was going to Lottie's in the Adirondacks. A decision made five minutes ago. She'd seen the nascent data that the authorities hated, proving their chronic failure: thousands of annual emergency-room visits in New York City by women and girls who acknowledged being hurt by their partners, the tip of the iceberg. And then there were the homicides. The likeliest person to kill a woman was her husband or boyfriend. The only close second was her ex. Now that she allowed herself think about it, her fate was clear. The fucker was going to put her under his thumb. He was calling to check up, to make sure she was home alone. And if he couldn't control her he was going to think about making her a statistic. Dead by the Long Island Expressway. Strangled in her apartment. Beaten on a dark street until he broke the bones in her face.

Let him try to find her. He'd probably be less uncomfortable up north than in the upscale Huntington bar where he went looking for her that night two weeks ago, told by somebody that she was back. He might even fit with a certain redneck crowd. But if he made any trouble whatsoever up there, her aunt would put a load of buckshot in his ass. Which, as far as Alison was concerned, was what he deserved. Bastard. The whole affair was just so low class. So crude. How could her judgment have been that bad? How did she get here? Lottie, in her own words, didn't take guff from anyone. She didn't trust anyone either, except maybe her favorite niece, who was coming unannounced. Her aunt had recently moved full time to her cabin in the woods, the one you had to take a boat to get to. Lottie didn't have a phone there. No use for it. Didn't want one. Or company, for the most part, except for her two big dogs. Alison hoped she'd be welcome.

She left the apartment key on the table with a note, telling the woman who gave her the sublet to keep the security deposit. Alison left no forwarding address. She pulled the door shut behind her and dragged the duffel bag and suitcase down three flights of stairs and out the back door of the building. She avoided the elevator. She was terrified of riding down and having the doors open to Will. He would think nothing of buzzing another tenant to get in the streetside door.

The dark alley looked quiet. She thought Will had probably called her from his little house in Hempstead, where she lived for six months and where he held her prisoner in the bedroom the last night, after ripping the phone out of the wall. He was probably just sitting up late drinking beer. She hoped he was not calling from a pay phone in her neighborhood. They were all broken anyway. Another community service in Mayor Koch's New York. She saw a figure in the diffuse light at the alley entrance. She stopped and stood still in the shadows. The figure passed. She couldn't remember if she locked the door. If he went up and opened it, he would know she had just left.

She moved quickly down the alley and around the corner, dragging her bags another block to the Chambers Street subway. Nobody followed her down the station stairs. Two homeless men were curled up asleep in a corner. She wouldn't miss the smell and couldn't be bothered right now about the psychosis that probably put them there. They had their reasons. It was not her problem. Not anymore. Probably not ever.

She dropped a token in the turnstile—for the last time, she hoped—and went downstairs. It took fifteen minutes for the next uptown train to arrive, and by then there were three other people on the platform. None of them was Will. She worried that he would follow her here. If he appeared now, she'd probably fall down and cry. She imagined him pushing her off the platform onto the hot rail. She thought of the behavioral theory she'd come up with recently, one she thought would make a neat pop-psychology maxim: fear doesn't make cowards of people; it just makes them hate. Her professors would be disappointed. No analysis, no empirical studies, and no subtlety.

2

At Penn Station, Alison dragged her bags up the subway stairs and down the echoing corridor to the vast cavern where a few people lounged or slept in the waiting area. None looked like travelers. Only a few ticket windows were open at 4:04 a.m., and the board showed the next Albany train would depart in two hours. It would be empty northbound on a Thursday in May, but she bought her ticket in advance anyway from a clerk behind a glass window who didn't look up once and ran her mother's American Express card and took the signed slip without asking for identification or examining how well Alison forged her mother's signature. She didn't have the forty dollars. And this was an emergency of sorts.

She saw a uniformed cop wandering through the starkly lit expanse of the station and felt better. She dragged her bags to the waiting area, plopped in a chair, and stashed the ticket in her pocketbook. She counted the cash in her wallet and thought it might be just enough for the taxi from the Rensselaer train station to the Albany bus depot and maybe the bus ride to the Adirondacks. She rummaged further and found the envelope with Aunt Lottie's mailing address, a post-office box in Newcomb, a flyspeck just south of the High Peaks. Alison hadn't been back to Newcomb since spending three glorious summers there as a girl. She refused to go home the last time until her mother sent a sharply worded letter to Lottie. As far as Alison knew, she was never invited back. In fact, Lottie had invited her every summer, but her mother had always replied that Alison was unavailable and had other interests. When Aunt Lottie brought this up at Alison's high-school graduation, Alison's mother at first pretended not to hear and when pressed said she hadn't wanted her daughter to turn into some sort of wild ragamuffin.

Alison wondered what interests her mother had in mind. Was it in Alison's interest to witness the tension and arguments that would lead to her parents' divorce when she was in college? Like that did a lot of goddamned good. Maybe she had in mind those ludicrous family outings. With brisk efficiency, her mother used to pile all four kids and their father into the car to go to an arboretum or bottle museum or some other boring place, as if this was what families were supposed to do. During the drive, her mother would narrate brightly from a brochure. Apart from those outings, Alison didn't see her father that much. He kept to himself and on weeknights always came home late from the city. How Aunt Charlotte, the unmarried woodswoman, and Dolores, the executive's fertile wife on Long Island's Gold Coast, could be sisters, that was a mystery.

Alison couldn't keep an eye on all the entrances to the vast room in Penn Station, so she slunk low in the chair and watched the one she'd come in from the subway. Three rough-looking men she'd noticed earlier had moved a few seats closer to her. They'd seemed to be drowsing before, and again now. The cop she saw wandering through the station when she first arrived was nowhere in sight. Suddenly it occurred to her that none of the half-dozen other people in the waiting area looked like upstanding citizens. The people who looked like professionals, with briefcases, newspapers, and coffee, had gathered under the electric board that listed the trains' arrivals and departures. They stood in a group, shifting and looking around, glancing at their watches, at the board, and at their newspapers and luggage. They were like grazing animals gathered together for safety on the African plain, while Alison had naively settled in among the hyenas. Or maybe she was just spooked by everything with Will. Then the man two seats away stood up, stretched, and sat one seat closer.

"Excuse me, miss," he said, leaning over.

"No," she said. Alison gripped her pocketbook, stood, grabbed her bags, and walked quickly past him, the duffel banging into the man's knees.

"Miss," he said. She didn't look at him, but hurried across the floor to the riders huddled beneath the board. She sidled into the middle of the group and kept her head down.

By the time her train arrived, a half-hour late, the station was getting crowded. Alison got in the first available car and took a seat in the rear, next to a window on the left and with the restroom wall behind her. She stuffed the duffel under her feet and laid the suitcase on the adjacent seat. She didn't want company. Soon after the half-empty train emerged from the tunnels, the conductor came by and punched her ticket.

The sun could be seen out the windows on the right, glimmering through the trees. Out her window Alison watched the wide, flat Hudson River. She began to relax, thinking she had escaped Will, and replayed everything that had happened. Her future was now a blank. She stared out the window a long while. When the door between cars opened, she was startled and looked up quickly, but it was just the conductor.

The train passed Haverstraw Bay, where the river was three miles across and looked as still as a lake, and Alison wondered how something as narrow, rocky, and wild as the upper Hudson could turn into this. She thought of Lottie's cabin in the timberlands on the east bank of the river, some three hundred miles north, and realized she wasn't quite sure how to get there.

3

Wallace Lafleur woke at first light, sat for a moment on the edge of his loft bed, legs dangling, and watched the contours of the sky form above the mountains. The windows along the back of his house on the outskirts of Lake Placid faced south. Two rows of large panes from one side to the other allowed the room to be bathed in light, a blessing in the short days of the long winter and a delight in the long warm days of summer. On this May morning, he figured it was about 6 a.m., give or take, but that didn't make any difference. He had no appointments, no clients to meet, and no guests in the front of the house, his bed-and-breakfast. There was the next day's raft trip to pack for, seven young women who'd just graduated from college and were rewarding themselves with a little Adirondack adventure. He wondered if any of them would be pretty, thought it was a good bet that some of them would be, and recalled his own rules. He would, of course, be friendly and welcoming, even flirt if any were inclined to be flirted with, and try to read them like he read the river, for the nuances, the hidden rocks, the eddies, the things to avoid, and make it fun.

Wallace didn't hit on clients, absolutely not, and he had to tell his friend Donny not to do it the first time he rowed the second raft. He reminded his friend that in post-feminist 1989, the only interest that was welcome was interest that was welcome. In short, it was the same as the river, which will tell you what it's doing, but you have to pay attention, like everything else in nature and society. And he was pretty sure he understood one thing that was true about relationships. Women choose. Men who thought or behaved otherwise, which was most of them, who imposed themselves and insisted, they were finally, fundamentally wrong, and unnatural. You could see the evidence in bent relationships all over, which he wanted no part of and didn't have time for. He got chosen often enough, and every day was an adventure. A joyful one, he decided for maybe the ten-thousandth time since he came to the Adirondacks almost two decades earlier to live this life on his own chosen terms.

"How do we do it?" he mused. He jumped down from the loft, pulled on jeans and a fleece shirt, pushed his long black hair back behind his ears, and walked out the door and over the dewy grass and then into the side door of the partitioned house. He splashed water on his face, smoothed his beard, made coffee, and went out onto the high deck to smell the woods and watch the sun rise over the Great Range. It would be another splendid day. He went back inside, sliced some fruit and put it into yogurt, added cereal, and stepped outside again to eat breakfast. Afterward he did the dishes, including a wine glass he used the night before while watching the cascade of stars, and started to think of all the things he needed to do in the days ahead. He brushed his teeth, put on his aviator sunglasses, grabbed a pen and legal pad, and for the next two hours drank coffee on the deck, looked at the High Peaks, and made a list. When he was done, he sat back, his mind clear of worries and distractions. He sensed something good was coming his way. And yet he never let himself forget that trouble might lie around the next bend.

4

With the easy rocking of the train, Alison dozed, her head resting against the window. She didn't see the old fortress of West Point, which, she once read, Benedict Arnold tried to sell to the British to support his love affair with a woman beyond his means, turning himself from American hero to traitor. She missed Storm King Mountain, where, Lottie told her, the Hudson River fishermen beat back a ConEd power plant and jump-started the modern environmental movement. She woke briefly in Poughkeepsie, and then passing through Kingston she emerged from a dream about her father, the first one in long time. She had many dreams about him just after he died, but not in a while. When she dreamed of him they were always having a conversation, and it was always about something happening in her life. He told her the most unexpected and helpful things. And this time again, it brought some clarity and peace, and since she missed him in person so much it felt good to be with him. She wondered if the bright sunshine inspired the dream. He loved summertime as much as she did, and they were sitting in a garden, one of his gardens at Cold Spring Harbor, where he could make anything grow.

William Reade had been a corporate executive in Manhattan, with a Ph.D. in chemistry, but he liked his gardens. In summertime, for no occasion at all, he would call a bunch of friends and let them know he was up for a game of croquet. The lawn game would cross one or two of his eight acres, with the cart of cocktails nearby. He played with a cigar in his mouth, listening, or perhaps not, to everyone bragging about their prowess in this silly game. About one-third of the way through he would order everyone to switch partners based on an algorithm he'd think up, like everyone with white shoes must now pair up with someone whose hair was a different color from theirs. Typically it matched the leader with the loser.

In winter, it was billiards in the back room that overlooked the lawn, on the large antique table he'd taken from the country club for free in exchange for getting the thing out of there and then refinished. On New Year's Eve, it was a black-tie affair, where women in fabulous cocktail dresses shot pool and played darts with their elegantly turned-out husbands who arrived in white silk scarves and cashmere overcoats. The women looked like birds of paradise, shiny, sequined, dresses cut down to there or up to here. Alison's dress was always black and backless and short, with very high heels, accented by long, dangling earrings and bracelets and French perfume, a flower in her hair from one of the bouquets, placed strategically in her swept-up mane. He'd invite fifty people, and seventy or eighty would come. Loud, boisterous, big-band music, champagne, an open bar, first-rate caterers. Raucous and fabulous. For a few years, in her late teens and early twenties, it was Alison's favorite evening. Every year she brought a different boyfriend. Evenings that should never end. Alas, they did. But they came back with the dream, the remembrance and feeling.

While her father was a humorous and resourceful storyteller, in the dreams he was taciturn, as he was usually when important things were being discussed. He mainly nodded and listened to Alison tell him all that troubled her. He said it was okay, nothing really to get upset about. That innocent, wide-eyed part of her life was over. She wasn't a girl anymore. It wasn't good or bad. It just meant she couldn't be the same person that she was before.

Just as she was waking up, reluctantly, under the Kingston bridge with the train stopping in increments, bouncing her gently, she asked him whom she would be now. He smiled and said he didn't know exactly, but he was quite sure that she would be older.

When the door opened, she bolted fully awake. A few new passengers straggled in noisily from the Kingston station. The problem was that her father was dead, and there was nothing he could do to protect her. She counted her money again and knew she didn't have enough for a bus ticket to the Adirondacks, even if there was service to Newcomb. She barely had enough for a cab ride from Rensselaer to the Trailways station across the river. She thought about panhandling, asking respectable-looking strangers for money or a ride, or hitchhiking. Instead she would make a call from a pay phone. And wait.

5

Lottie pulled up to the train station in a dark-blue pickup truck, with two German shorthaired pointers in the backseat, their noses poking out of the partly lowered windows. Alison, sitting on her suitcase, her back pressed to the station's outer wall, where she could see everyone coming and going, knew right away it was Lottie: the slow-moving truck, the cascade of white hair, the dogs, and the voice from inside the truck shouting at them to get down and behave. This was the woman she'd come to for refuge, the ornery one who didn't tolerate fools gladly.

Alison carried her bags to the truck and started to heft them into the truck bed. Lottie rolled down the passenger-side window.

"Put them in here, girl," Lottie said. "I'm not going to go chasing them when they bounce out the back."

Alison opened the door, and Lottie yelled at the dogs to stay in the small backseat, where there wasn't much room with the suitcase and the duffel. Alison got in front, and the dogs nosed her, their stub tails wagging.

"You leave her alone, now," Lottie said.

"Is that Einstein?" Alison asked.

"No. Einstein died a few years ago. That's DaVinci and Marx."

"You mean like Groucho?"

"Karl, Groucho, it's about the same. They're all comedians."

Alison took a long look at her aunt. Still striking, though smaller than she remembered, but with the same fierce gaze, one that seemed to carry some kindness for her niece.

"I'm sorry to make you come all this way," Alison said.

"There aren't many things that would make me come down here. I think the last time was when I took you to the train. What was that, ten years ago?"

"Twelve."

"I guess it took you a while to think about coming back. I didn't realize I'd scared you that much the last time."

"Aunt Lottie, I'm so sorry." She faced her aunt. "You know for the longest time I didn't know I was invited back. And then life got complicated."

"I know your mother never really wanted you up here. What changed her mind now?" Lottie kept the truck in park, the engine running.

"I called her to see if she could get in touch with you. I was coming one way or another. It's not up to her. I'm not a girl anymore. I hoped you'd let me in."

"Lucky for you this was my day to go to the store in Newcomb. Otherwise I wouldn't have received the message and known to come get you. They don't like to come down to the cabin to deliver my messages these days. And frankly, I don't want them to." Lottie studied her niece's face. "Are you in trouble of some kind?"

"Maybe."

"Are you sick or pregnant?"

"No."

"Well, that's good. Because the medical care up my way isn't much, unless you travel a distance. I'm good with mild ailments, but not much else."

Lottie put the truck in drive and pulled away from the station.

At the first traffic light in Rensselaer, she looked at Alison, who was staring out the window. "Are you in trouble with the law? Don't care. I just want to know whether to expect the sheriff or the state police."

"No. If it's okay, I'll tell you about it tomorrow. It's just a guy."

"What did he do?"

"He wouldn't let me go." Alison took a sudden deep gulp of air and began to cry, her shoulders shaking. The dogs stood and tried to nuzzle her from the backseat. "I've never been so afraid."

Lottie scolded the dogs to lie down and kept driving.

"Well, the shotgun in the back window is loaded. It's pump action. Five shells. Assuming you remember how to use it, it's there."

As they crossed the Hudson into Albany, they could see five modern skyscrapers towering over century-old buildings, a marble monument to the power and ego of Nelson Rockefeller, the former governor. The sight of the office plaza and the nearby statehouse put Lottie in a foul mood.

"This has been a season for scoundrels and rascals," Lottie said. "And

I'm about as inclined as I've ever been to put an assful of buckshot into all of them."

Alison didn't say anything.

"Sometime when you're ready, maybe you'll tell me your troubles. And I'll tell you mine," Lottie said, and got more silence. "But there's my river, and even down here, with all the concrete and exhaust and whatever else they throw at it and in it, it's still a river. Look, there are ducks on the far shore. I can't tell what kind from here."

As they drove north along the river, Alison watched the scenery with little interest. Lottie drove at a steady 55 mph, paying no mind to all the cars passing her. After several miles, they headed west and got on the Northway, the interstate that goes to Canada. Soon the traffic thinned out. An hour later, they passed the sign for the Adirondack Park and rolled up into the landscape of low green mountains.

6

Lafleur's list was fairly short since he had staffing for the weekend and had just retired his eighth bank loan, leaving seven to go. The most important thing was to find someone to manage the B&B and do the regular drives and supply runs for the rafting trips. It had been a good spring and was shaping up to be a busy summer, and that would mean lots of phone calls to find friends who could work a day here or there. He really did need somebody.

Since Susan left, he'd been reluctant to hire a replacement. She was a good worker, even more organized than Wallace, kept meticulous accounts, and charmed the clients. At the end of their rafting trips, she always put out a nice lunch near the takeout in the hamlet of North River. The white wine was perfectly chilled; the buffet of deli food, salads, breads, and home-baked desserts was fresh and attractive; the soup, coffee, and cocoa were hot and plentiful. She kept the B&B immaculate and well stocked. She'd been in catering, and was petite, cheerful, and full of energy. She came to work for him last fall after Carol, his longtime manager, had her second child and left to focus on raising her boys.

In October and November, in between guiding hunters from downstate and drinking red wine with them in the evenings around the B&B's hearth, Wallace found himself hanging around the kitchen, where Susan cooked hearty breakfasts and dinners for the guests and packed their lunches. The night she came to his room, which was separated from the rest of the house, with its own entrance, he wasn't entirely surprised. It was the best winter he could remember, though there weren't many guests for backcountry skiing and snowshoeing. She brought light and energy and a stronger sense of purpose to his world, where sometimes, especially in winter, he'd drift. Susan was passionate and smart. He hoped it would go on indefinitely. She introduced him to her parents, New Yorkers with a summer place on Upper Saranac Lake. After ten years of working at high-end restaurants and catering corporate events, Susan needed a break. She was planning her next move, maybe to launch her own business, when she decided to answer Wallace's ad and slow things down for a few months. Once on the job, she saw possibilities unlooked for. There was talk of marriage, and reorganizing the loans, and a side business in catering, and joining the chamber of commerce, maybe even taking up golf and joining the country club. Those were mainly her suggestions. On Wallace's birthday she bought him a blazer, like the one her father wore to dinner the evening they met him at the country club.

The night Wallace told her he wasn't really convinced these were the things he wanted to do, Susan cried.

"I'm ready to give you everything!" she said.

"So am I," Wallace replied. "Here it is. Just stay. I'm so easy."

"But you don't want to get married." It was an accusation.

"Well, not if it means joining the country club." He thought that was kind of funny.

She slapped him. He saw it coming and let it land. She hit hard for 105 pounds. It was a breaking point, and they both knew it. And they both knew that he let it happen. She had a lot of angry questions. How can you do that? How can you be that insensitive? Why do you hate me? He'd never even considered the last one a possibility until she brought it up.

Wallace went into the bathroom, locked the door, and for a while thought she'd calm down and he'd come back out to discuss it. But she started to sound even angrier. He climbed out the window, an old trick from his boyhood in Utica, where he was always slipping off into the woods at the end of the street. He stepped quietly into his equipment room and grabbed a coat, gloves, hat, and heavy boots. There was still snow under the trees, though the mud season was on and he had several whitewater trips coming up. He took a flashlight, too, and disappeared into the forest. He walked quietly all night, dozed on a rock outcropping in the sun the next morning. When he went back, Susan was gone. So were her clothes. She didn't break anything, didn't take anything of his, though she had access to his accounts, and the rifles and shotgun were still on the wall. She left one short note in her neat handwriting: "You know where to reach me." She didn't leave her set of keys to his house and truck. He felt the slight swelling on his cheek and thought about calling. He didn't think much of getting hit. But it broke faith. And that was enough to let him end it.

7

Alison slept on the ride north. She woke to an empty pickup and panicked for a moment until she realized they were parked outside the general store in Newcomb, which hadn't changed in twelve years. Lottie came out with a bag of groceries, followed by the dogs. They walked down the road and loaded everything in Lottie's little aluminum boat with the outboard motor, which she'd left tied to a post near the boat ramp. As they traveled down the Hudson, Alison sat toward the middle, behind the dogs, and later could hardly remember the trip. When they got off the river, the dogs ran ahead. She and Lottie pulled the outboard into the edge of the woods and chained it to a tree.

"If somebody tries to steal it I'll chop their hands off," Lottie said. Alison wondered if she was joking and decided she was. Mostly.

There was an old aluminum canoe nearby, chained to nothing. The cabin stood about a hundred yards from the river, in a small clearing behind some trees. It had an open southern exposure with a big latticed window but sat snug against a stand of maple and birch on the north side. There was a plank porch, where Lottie, an ornithologist, worked at her typewriter when it was warm and sunny, with journals, photographs, and books on a table next to her. When it was cold or rainy, she worked indoors by the wood stove. The cabin had two rooms, a well for water, indoor plumbing, and a propane hot-water tank.

Alison had a slight cough and felt chilled and feverish. Lottie put her in the smaller room, the bedroom, on the soft mattress in a sleeping bag, under quilts. She slept there with the dogs snuggled against her as if they sensed her need for comfort and protection. She woke twelve hours later, damp and still tired. Lottie fed her vegetable soup and freshly baked crusty bread. Alison stayed in bed for another day, refusing to think about anything. When unsettling thoughts intruded, she went back to sleep. She found comfort in breathing the clean air, listening to the breeze in the trees, and hearing her aunt's occasional footfalls. Her fever broke.

On the third day, she woke to the smell of breakfast. Lottie made pancakes, bacon, and stronger-than-usual coffee and laid everything out on the hewn wooden table. Alison looked around, at the log walls, the wood stove, the steel sink, and the window with the view of the forest, at Lottie's clear blue eyes and lined face. Little had changed since her summers here. She saw her old recurve bow leaning against one of the two straight-back chairs.

"My bow," Alison said. "I wondered what happened to her."

"So that thing is a her. I remember."

Alison ran her hands over its smooth contours. The string dangled from one end.

"Do you think the string is still good?"

"I bought that one the other day," Lottie said. "It works just fine."

Alison pulled the top of the bow down, attached the string at the other tip, and let it stretch taut. She felt the heft, ran her finger down the string, gripped the bow, and pulled the string back with three fingers until she could feel the thirty-five pounds of pressure on her fingertips.

"Where have you been?"

Her aunt had given it to her and taught her archery as a girl. She took it with her when she went exploring in the forest. She had small sharp field points on her arrows, instead of the large, lethal broadhead. In Lottie's view, the field points were safer for everyone and probably still enough to drive off a bear, a man, or anything else. Alison had aimed the bow at various animals, after waiting furtively in her makeshift blinds, but she shot only one. She had heard a ruckus in a tree and saw something that at first she couldn't believe, a squirrel on a high branch, biting a mourning dove, which was frantically flapping its wings. A strange and terrible sight to the girl. "Stop it," she yelled. Then she drew an arrow and took steady aim at the squirrel's thick body. The bird dropped off the branch, fluttered to earth, hopped a while, and flew off. The squirrel fell to the ground and died. Alison buried the squirrel and the arrow. "It's your own fault," she said by way of eulogy. She put the bow away. It was almost September anyway. Although she liked the idea of hunting, she realized she didn't like killing things. She still felt that way.

"I figured it's time you got out a little bit," Lottie said. "I got you six arrows. They're used, but they'll do."

When Alison went to bed that evening, she laid the unstrung bow on the floor beside her. The dogs again snuggled against her. Over the next few days, she did little else but sleep, eat, and observe the forest from the front porch. Then, feeling fully recovered, she woke one morning with an inspiration. Taking burlap sacks piled in the closet, Alison made an effigy, with head, arms, legs, and torso cut and roughly stitched together. She filled it with twigs and leaves, and on the outside she pinned a piece of paper on which she had scrawled one word in big letters: Will. She felt a little alarmed at her action, as if he would know what she was doing and find a way to pay her back.

"What are you making?" Lottie asked when it was nearly finished.

"A target."

She studied her niece and the effigy. "Anybody you know?"

"He was my boyfriend," Alison said. "He was nice for a while. But then he changed. He cheated on me, and he wouldn't let me go. He refused to let me go. And then he became my stalker. That's the word for it now."

"You can tell me about it," Lottie said. "There's not much that surprises me."

Alison told the story from the beginning, when she first met Will. She spoke slowly, handling the bow the entire time, running her fingers over the smooth fiberglass. As Alison talked, Lottie mixed up a batch of bread dough and then covered the mixing bowl with a cloth to let it rise. Afterward she sat next to Alison and listened without interrupting.

"Well, then," Lottie finally said. "I think a target's a good idea. It'll get you in the mood in case he does show up here."

Alison laughed for the first time in what seemed like months. She hung the effigy in a maple tree near the river and began target practice. It came back quickly, the feeling, the sense of skill. She was much stronger than the girl who had killed the squirrel. The first shot went low, striking the burlap just below the torso. She found that amusing. The next shots went higher.

Lottie watched the archery practice the next afternoon and brought out the double-barreled shotgun from under the bed. She wanted to make sure Alison still knew how to load and shoot it. Lottie shared her own story about her wildlife studies for the Department of Environmental Conservation and the Adirondack Park Agency. Many people up here resented the State of New

York and the restrictions that kept them from doing whatever they pleased on their land—a big change from the old days, which weren't that long ago. Some nut had actually shot at a car carrying park agency workers. "Can you believe that?" she said. There was a lot of shouting at public meetings and veiled threats. One local official slugged an Earth First demonstrator, a long-haired kid, right in front of a state trooper and got away with it. The worst was when somebody set Lottie's barns on fire. After months of sleeping with her gun, afraid they were coming back to burn her house down too, she left for her summer cabin more or less permanently. Her account was light on details, as these were sore subjects, but she wanted Alison to know where things stood.

"If that's what passes for civilization, I said to hell with it," Lottie said. "I didn't really want to have to shoot anybody. But if you have to you have to."

"Aren't we a pair?" Alison replied. She loaded and unloaded the shotgun twice, careful to keep the barrel pointed away from the dogs and her aunt. She moved the safety on and off. She aimed the gun at the effigy, then lowered it. She put the safety on, unloaded the gun, and handed it back.

8

Most of Wallace Lafleur's raft trips began on the Indian River, a little below the dam on Lake Abanakee. Each morning the town released water from the dam, creating a "bubble" that the rafting outfitters rode through the Hudson Gorge. Lafleur tried to fill each of his boats with eight clients, sitting two by two. The clients did the paddling; Lafleur sat in the rear, using his paddle as a rudder, his feet hooked under a strap for security. He had acquired enough wetsuits over the years to outfit all his customers, but the suits were optional. Everyone was required everyone to wear flotation vests and helmets—except him. His black hair flew loose in the wind, his aviators held on with a strap behind his head. Although the clients signed injury waivers, Lafleur was a stickler for safety. He always checked that vests were cinched properly and helmets were secure. Before the trip, he gave a lecture about safety. Once on the water, he cheerfully barked instructions to paddle on the left, or on the right, or all together, to paddle hard or to back-paddle, or to rest. It kept the raft moving downstream and out of trouble.

The seventeen-mile course ran from the Indian into the Hudson and through the gorge, passing the spectacular limestone cliff called Blue Ledge. It ended by the road in North River, where Lafleur's assistant would set up lunch under tent pavilions on the grass. The rivers boasted some serious whitewater, with some big drops and tight channels rushing between boulders. In spring, with the mountains' runoff, the water ran higher and faster, as wild as anywhere in the country. In twenty years Lafleur had seen maybe ten clients bounce out of the raft, and he got them all back quickly and unhurt. Some outfitters deliberately hit the waves as hard as they could to see who'd go flying. Lafleur didn't do that. He'd never flipped a boat. It was a great trip without the stunts, stunningly beautiful, far from civilization, the mountain water clean and wild and cold. Instead he tried to teach people how to read the river, which was different every time. Sure, they got splashed and bucked. That was part of the fun. They might also stop to take a swim in a refreshing pool. At the end of the trip, they changed into dry clothes and enjoyed a hearty lunch. Lafleur had few dissatisfied customers. Most felt they had left their troubles for a day and acquired something—a little skill, a heightened sense of possibility.

His favorite trip was out of Newcomb, about a dozen miles north of the usual put-in. It was a two-day excursion, all on the Hudson. At first, the river was not terribly rough or fast. He'd paddle through timber-company tracts and camp on a state-owned spit of land at the confluence of the Cedar River, a remote and enchanting place. On the second day he'd go through the gorge.

In May he took a lone executive on the overnight trip, the raft equipped with two long oars. Lafleur rowed facing forward, so he could read the water, sometimes pushing the oars, sometimes drifting with the current. The executive, whose name was Eldridge, fished for trout and bass.

"Your name sounds a little like Elrond the elf king," Wallace had told him the night before in an attempt to break the man's sour mood. "I noticed that when you called to make the reservation."

"I never heard that before."

"It's from the Tolkien trilogy. The books."

Eldridge was drinking single-malt scotch by the hearth at the B&B, while Lafleur kept the glass filled and the fire stoked and talked about the trip. "This is a place where extraordinary things can and do happen. You can decide who you are, and you can be that. It's all possible here."

He added, "Even the dark lord can't do anything to Tom Bombadil." And he laughed. Wallace sometimes jokingly likened himself to Tolkien's original, perpetual natural man, and he tried to explain it to the distracted executive.

Lafleur brought out his worn paperback copies of the novels, and Eldridge flipped through them but mostly watched the fire while Wallace grilled steaks and vegetables on his back deck. Eldridge woke in the morning starting to feel disconnected from the cares of his contracting business. He began calling Wallace "Bombadoo" and once referred to himself jokingly as "Elrond."

"All right, your majesty," Wallace replied. "Let's find out just how much magic you've got."

They drove to Newcomb in the pickup, pulling the crimson raft on a trailer. After unloading, Wallace packed the raft and parked the truck. It was midmorning when they launched. For the first mile, the river was wide and flat. The older man soon began casting for fish, and he asked Wallace how he came here.

Lafleur told him about the juvenile delinquents that he used to take, on behalf of the state, on monthlong outings in the wilderness. He always liked the woods—he had done a lot of hunting and some mountaineering—and he thought it would be good. But the kids were wearing.

"When you're in the neighborhood the strongest person is in charge, in control. When I'd get these kids, I'd say, 'This is what we're going to do.' They'd think, 'Not really. Because we're not totally convinced you're in charge here. Because we're taking over this gig.' Every outing there was a fight, sometimes a few, until I proved that I was in charge. And that was a temporary thing. Some of the kids learned something about the woods and about nature and getting along. They went on and did fine. Others were just going to go back home and try to be top dog again."

They drifted for a few minutes. Eldridge said that was kind of like his business, where he had to be top dog. There was no way around it. He asked Lafleur how he got out of it.

"It occurred to me that fighting got squarely in the way of every good thing, and I didn't want to anymore. I gave up karate for tai chi. I went with the flow. I quit working for the state and sailed a friend's boat all the way down the Intracoastal Waterway to Florida. At the end, I threw my watch and keys into the ocean. I was done with that world."

"Really?" Eldridge reeled in his line and looked at the guide. "Then what?"

"I returned to the mountains with a little money in the bank and an idea that I had all the outdoor guiding skills but needed a different clientele. I advertised as a mountaineer and teacher of technical climbing and survival skills. The business that came in was for a hunting guide and whitewater trips. And fishing. And here we are. "

They were beginning to hear rills of whitewater when they saw the young woman with the bow. They stopped what they were doing and watched, unnoticed at first by the archer.

She was tall and lean, wearing denim shorts, T-shirt, and hiking boots, with her long hair pulled into a bronze ponytail. She faced a human effigy twenty yards away that was hanging by the neck from a branch, its back resting against the tree trunk. She shot three arrows at the effigy, pausing to evaluate each shot, then carefully drawing and aiming the next arrow. Lafleur noticed that she used her entire back, with good form, deliberately. Each arrow hit with a thwack, sticking the figure's torso to the tree trunk.

"Would you look at that," Eldridge said softly.

Wallace had begun rowing gently against the current, holding them near the center of the channel. The woman drew a fourth arrow. It flew straight, hitting the effigy in the center of the head. She walked to the tree and pulled the arrows out. She looked upriver and saw them. Her hand tightened on the bow. Eldridge waved, but she only looked at them and walked into the forest.

"What was that?" Eldridge said. "Not very friendly."

"Diana the huntress, I'd say."

"Let's hope she doesn't get it in her head to shoot this way."

"They're probably field points. Target arrows. But she can shoot. No doubt about that," Lafleur said. He scanned the forest to see if she were watching them, but he didn't see any sign of her. He resumed rowing downstream, and the river soon narrowed and picked up speed.

"I'd say Lottie has a visitor," Lafleur said.

"Who's Lottie?"

"She has a cabin up in there on twenty-two acres. She leases it from the timber company. It was a hunting camp once. It's posted, though. And if you surprise Lottie expect to be greeted by two big dogs and a shotgun. Unless she knows you to be a friend."

"It sounds like your Adirondacks aren't all that friendly."

"Just the opposite," Wallace said. "Adirondack women are strong, rugged, sweet-natured, and willing. They'll try anything, and they'll cure anything that ails you. Of course, those that aren't friendly, they've got their reasons."

The next afternoon, Donny drove the truck and trailer from Newcomb to the takeout at North River, while Carol brought Eldridge's shiny oversize pickup down so he could go straight back to Delaware. The businessman tipped Lafleur an extra $400 on top of the $1,200 fee for the two-day rafting trip.

"See you around, Bombadoo," he said. "Keep a couple days open for me next year."

"Absolutely. You can count on it. Let me know when so I can put you in the calendar. There are a lot of good days in the fall, too."

Though the others were in the truck with him, Wallace drove twenty-five miles out of their way and stopped at the general store in Newcomb to inquire generally about Lottie, which he'd been meaning to do. He learned that the archer was her niece from New York City, that her name was Alison. She had made an impression on him with her long legs and sharp gaze. He would say later that he was intrigued, though it would have been equally reasonable to be afraid.

9

Lafleur had another overnight trip at the end of the month, six new college graduates with degrees in physical therapy, three named Megan and one bringing a boyfriend along. Carol, who still guided for him sometimes, rowed the second raft with all the gear: tents, sleeping bags, coolers of food, and other supplies.

The women in Wallace's raft were all twentysomething, energetic and inclined to laughter. It promised to be a fun couple of days, though Carol was cranky, having to leave her two young sons with their father. She grumbled more when Wallace suggested they look in on Lottie. He said he wanted to see how she was doing after that trouble on her farm.

"She's an old dingbat," Carol said. "Always stirring things up."

"Now, Carol, one day when you're a little older somebody's going to say that about you. And you know what I'm going to say? That's it's not true. Not about you. Not completely."

He left the others on the bank and headed into the woods. It was overcast. He went quietly and knocked on the cabin door, which set the dogs barking. Until then, they hadn't heard him.

"Who is it?" Lottie called through the door.

"Wallace Lafleur."

Her face appeared at the window. She saw him and a moment later unlatched the door.

"Well, to what do I owe the honor?"

"Darling Lottie, you know I can't pass this stretch of river without stopping to see the one and only true woman of the Adirondacks."

"You tell me that same lie every time."

"Yes I do. And I believe that eventually you'll take me at my word."

"Fat chance of that," Lottie replied. She still sounded gruff, though he could tell she wasn't unhappy to see him. "You'd probably try to talk the birds out of the trees just to see if they're that foolish."

"I wouldn't, Lottie, and do you know why? Because you're looking out for them. And I'm afraid they'd tell you what I was up to."

"No good as usual. And what are you up to?"

"Just saying hello. I'd heard about your trouble and knew you were back down here. Semi-permanently is how I heard it."

"Some people talk too much." Her cheerfulness left.

"That's true. But I don't. Not about important things. How are you?"

"I'm all right. But tell me something. What kind of people burn your barns?"

"I don't know."

Lottie frowned, lost in thought. In a study for the park agency, she discovered that rare migratory birds nested in timberlands that some big developers wanted to subdivide for vacation homes. The study helped persuade the agency to block the project, earning her the enmity of people used to the old unregulated Adirondacks. For the most part, the malice and threats were anonymous, and in her eyes both frightening and cowardly.

Still, there were those in the mountains who truly resented the interference, as they called it, which began little more than a decade earlier, in the 1970s, with the creation of the park agency and all the new regulations and the emergence of environmentalists. So she left the farmhouse in Jay, where she preferred to spend winters, closed and locked. She wasn't sure when she would go back.

"Need anything?" he asked.

"No."

"You're okay alone?"

"I'm not alone." Lottie swung open the door. Behind her, sitting with a book, her feet propped on a log near the wood stove, was the young woman Lafleur had seen with the bow.

"Hello."

She glanced up briefly.

"This is my niece Alison. Alison, this is Wallace Lafleur. He's a guide on my river."

Alison glanced up again, nodded, and didn't say anything.

"I think we met almost. I believe it was last week. I saw you shooting arrows into a man."

"Unfortunately it was a straw man." She recognized him, the wild-haired, bearded rafter with the old guy who looked like he'd been outfitted straight from the Orvis catalog.

"Some people do feel that way," he replied. "What I was thinking, Lottie, is that I have an extra seat in my raft today and was wondering if in case you had an inclination to some company, you'd like to occupy it. Spend the night by the Cedar River, shoot the gorge tomorrow, you'll be home for supper tomorrow night. As my guest. I'd just enjoy it if you were your usual fascinating self with the girls I've got on this trip. You could teach them everything there is to know about birds."

"I couldn't do that. Alison's here. Besides, I've got a report due to the state two weeks ago."

"You sure? You were a big hit before."

"No, not this time."

"All right," Wallace said. "Alison, would you like to come?"

"Me? No. I don't know anything about rafting. And not much about birds."

Wallace took a moment and looked at her, thinking of what to say next. Half his reason for stopping was to meet her. "See, the challenge is my clients just left civilization; they've turned on the television, and the only entertainment is me. Now, I'm pretty entertaining sometimes. But we've got about thirty hours to go. My usual colleague, Donny, is not here. They're nice girls, and we've got the seat. Lottie would be ideal. If you're not an ornithologist like your aunt, what do you do?"

"I'm a student. I study psychology."

"Great. You can psychoanalyze us for entertainment and solve our problems. Not that anybody can have many on a day like this."

"I don't think so."

But the truth was her aunt had begun to find Alison, after a week, someone in need of something to do. She shot arrows, cooked, ate, slept, sunbathed, and read. Lottie thought Alison should go and would not hear otherwise.

"Why? What else are you going to do?" she asked.

"What I've been doing. I don't want to."

"What you can't do is sit here feeling sorry for yourself. And you can't spend the summer just climbing trees and reading books."

Lottie's words stung, more so that she said them in front of a stranger.

"Fine." She stuffed some warm clothes into Lottie's smaller backpack, rolled up a sleeping bag, and followed Lafleur out silently.

He gave her an extra wetsuit from the second raft. Rather than return to the cabin, she took it into the woods and pulled it on, after sliding off her jeans and flannel shirt. She stuffed her clothes in the backpack, which Wallace placed inside a waterproof bag. He handed her a life vest and helmet. She put on the vest first, leaving the straps dangling. She clipped them and made them snug when he mentioned they should be and stepped forward as if to do it. He had her sit in the back of the first raft near him, gave her a paddle, and ran quickly through the paddle commands. Introduced as a psychologist and prodded by the others, she reluctantly began talking after they pushed off. She learned all the girls had graduated from a Catholic college. The physical therapists had some background in psychology.

"Teach us something," Wallace said when they came to a stretch of flat water. Alison talked about the fundamental error of attribution, how people tend to excuse their own behavior, finding reasons for whatever they did, and seeing character flaws in others when they do precisely the same thing.

"So it's like when you don't paddle very hard, you're all just lily-dippers," Lafleur said. "And when I don't paddle very hard it's because I'm distracted by thinking deep thoughts."

"Something like that."

"Let's test the theory," he said, and called out some of the commands he'd taught them. They paddled hard as they bounced through a series of curling waves, water splashing over the bow. The women laughed and whooped. Then the river slowed again, and he told them to rest.

"There are no lily-dippers in this raft!" he announced. "I call that the fundamental theory of contribution. All dancing on the river together. How do we do it?"

He added, more softly, "With style and grace."

Alison wondered if he were mocking her. Probably not, she told herself. She started talking about cognitive dissonance, the holding in the mind of incompatible beliefs. The conversation and the raft slowed.

"So you can reconcile everything?" one of the Megans asked.

"Sure," Alison replied. "It's like Salome and John the Baptist. You all know that story, right? She asked for his head, and then it came on a platter. Richly deserved, no doubt. But if not–oh, well! La-di-da, these things happen, and sometimes we get carried away, we women."

Alison looked at Wallace, and they all laughed. Except the one girl's boyfriend, who looked perplexed and who didn't think it funny at all.

10

T here were things they wouldn't recall clearly later and some details they disagreed on—for example, exactly how Alison came to work for Wallace and who suggested it first. They were both clear on one thing: Carol had been ornery and difficult the entire time rowing the second raft, which she almost flipped twice. She was angry with Wallace and spoke little to the clients. When they reached the campsite, she rowed the second raft hard toward the bank and called for the others to pull her ashore. She then stepped out of the raft before it was secured, fell into the water, and came up snarling and scolding the young women, who had given the raft an extra tug after she said to stop.

"Goddamn it, girls, pay attention!" she barked.

Carol was Alison's height and looked sturdier. She was a strong woman who never shed the weight from her second baby. She was usually cheerful but hadn't wanted to do the overnight. She had to leave the boys in the care of their father, from whom she was lately separated, and hadn't rowed a raft in a while. But Lafleur had prevailed on her to take this trip for him. He didn't have anyone else. He was making almost $1,500 for the two days. In her black wetsuit, glowering, Carol looked fierce and miserable. Like an angry bear, Alison thought. She didn't know what she would do if Carol challenged her. Nevertheless, she stood in front of her and replied coolly, "We're just trying to help."

Wallace did not witness the incident. He and two of the young women had been gathering dried wood and pine needles and twigs for a fire. When he returned, he sensed the chill in the air. Carol stomped off among the trees to change into dry clothes. At Alison's direction, the others pulled the supply raft farther onto the shore and unloaded it. She then helped them put up the tents. She wanted to prove she was no freeloader.

That evening, Carol and Wallace made dinner, grilling chicken and corn on the fire. They broke out a few bottles of red wine, and Carol apologized to each of the clients and grudgingly to Alison. After dinner, Lafleur took out his guitar, strummed it softly, and told a few stories. Mostly, though, he stoked the fire. Alison slept in a tent with two girls with whom she especially hit it off. She nestled deep in her aunt's old sleeping bag. In her stay at the cabin, she had come to feel safe in its womblike embrace.

In the morning, Alison woke before the others and walked to the confluence of the Hudson and Cedar. She got there before dawn and sat in the dark at the water's edge, listening to the roar of the rivers. She felt their ancient force, water from the mountains heading to the sea. It was peaceful. The smell was clean, faintly metallic, different from that of the loamy woods. She breathed it in. She watched the water moving past, its dark rippling surface glistening under starlight, framed by the blackness of the forest. She imagined letting the river wash away her fear and sorrow, as much as it could bear, as much as she was willing to let go. Immediately, she dismissed this notion as self-directed suggestion. Still, she couldn't deny how she felt. And didn't want to. Forget that noise in her head, she thought. And everybody who ever put it there.

Wallace woke at first light. While he stirred the embers of the fire and made coffee, she sat on a log across from him and stared quietly at the flames. He pulled out skillets and fried bacon, eggs, and bread, which would soon attract the others. He filled an old metal coffee pot with water and coffee and set it on the fire.

"Did you sleep well?" he said.

"For a while. Then I sat by the river and watched the dawn. It's beautiful here. Do you come here a lot?"

"Maybe two or three times a season. When somebody wants to do an overnight. Some years more often." He added, "Thank you for your help."

"It's the least I could do. I'm not a paying customer, and the psychology wasn't all that interesting."

"That John the Baptist story was good."

"Did you think so? I hope you didn't take it too personally. It wasn't really about you, you know."

"Just men in general?"

"Some men. And you know, like my aunt, I'm what's known as frontally disinhibited."

"What does that mean?"

"I say what I think, often unedited."

Lafleur liked the way she'd taken charge and that she was direct. He also knew that Carol wasn't working out for the season and that Donny was trying to make music his full-time job and was often unavailable. Wallace needed somebody. He watched Alison through the roughest whitewater the second day, her ease, cheerfulness, laughter, and lack of fear. He learned that she had been a lifeguard and liked the water, including the ocean. Before the day was over Alison asked how you got to be a river guide, and Wallace asked her if she wanted a job. He explained it. It wasn't that glamorous, usually two or three outings a week during the season, mostly day trips. It meant putting on the lunch at the trip's end in North River, cleaning up, and ferrying the gear in his van. Also she would meet the groups in the morning and get them to sign waivers, outfit them in wetsuits, and collect their clothes to bring to the takeout.

He dropped her in Newcomb on the drive back. She thought about it for two days, talked about it with Lottie, whom she forgave for pushing her into the trip. She was broke, starting to get bored, and thought there were things she liked about Lafleur's approach, his apparent gentleness, and probably some things she could learn from him.

"How old are you?" she said, the afternoon she drove Lottie's pickup to his bed-and-breakfast. It was marked with a wooden sign on the far outskirts of Lake Placid.

"Thirty-eight. Why does it matter?"

"You're starting to be a graybeard."

It was true. There were flecks of gray in the short black beard that covered his face. He walked her around his five acres, showing her the equipment room, the vehicles, both rafts, the oars, paddles, wetsuits, oversize refrigerator, and the barn. They sat in his small office and bedroom at the back of the B&B, where she filled out employment and tax forms.

"Will you teach me to guide?" she asked.

Wallace looked at her and slowly nodded. "When there's time, we can get you started. Maybe by the end of the season you'll be able to row the second raft."

Alison felt slighted. "You think I'm a slow learner?"

"No. I don't. It takes a while to be good. See, the river can kill you. It doesn't very often, but it can. Certainly it can hurt you. And I promise my clients the best and safest rafting experience possible."

Alison finished filling out the forms and handed them to Wallace. "You might want to consider getting rid of the beard."

"And why is that?"

"Those girls on the trip thought you were cute. A couple even said you were handsome. But then they talked about the gray and wondered how old you were."

"It's not a secret," Wallace said.

"Well, if they just turned on the TV and you're the entertainment of the day, they'd probably like somebody they can dream on," Alison said. "And it's not their grandfather. As your new employee, I'd say that shaving would probably be good for business."

Wallace looked at her for a long time. "And what about you?"

"What about me?"

"I'd say denim shorts, dusty flip-flops or hiking boots, and either a tank top or long-sleeve flannel shirt with the tails tied above your waist. Hair tied back loose or just wild. More than half of my clients are men and boys. I'd call that the uniform of the Adirondack woman of their dreams."

"That's sexist, you know," she said.

"Is it?"

"You know it is."

"And here I thought I was just trying to be fair," he said. "And do what's best for business. You know, give everybody somebody they can dream on."

Over the first two weeks, they managed six day trips and began to figure out how to do things together. Neither one acted on the other's grooming advice, not right away. They did later on, without acknowledging why.

II

Will Palmer got up early, dressed, made himself coffee. He'd showered the night before and thrown his gym bag in the backseat of the car with a change of clothes and a toothbrush, thinking it was just possible he would reconnect and get lucky. He moved the .38-caliber revolver with its worn wooden grip from his pickup, where it was taped under the seat, to the Mustang. That was in case he was terribly unlucky. He didn't really expect that. Mainly he wanted to talk with Alison again. He'd been thinking about her a lot and wanted to see if he really felt that way and why. It was funny because he'd gotten kind of bored with her. She always liked to be attended to, fussed over, bought gifts, listened to as if everything she thought was interesting, a Gold Coast princess. But then he couldn't keep his mind off her once she was gone. He had an image of her in his head he couldn't shake, having a quality somebody once described as ethereal. He had to ask what that meant. Angelic, in a way. Though the thing he thought most about was the sex. That had seemed unattainable at first. So he was determined to try his luck with this girl, and it was pretty good. Surprising even. He told his friends it was like dating a lesbian. On their second date, she brought the U-Haul. He tried to tell his brother George, who didn't get the joke. Even after he explained it. Alison would have laughed, though he never told her. She would have been offended, probably, once she started thinking about it. She made no bones about wanting to move out of her mother's house. But she also wanted to be with him. Two or three times, she told him she loved him two or three times. He couldn't remember the exact circumstances. Now he wanted to see her. Just that. He knew there was still something there. How could there not be? That night he followed her, she just overreacted. She needed to calm down. Will bought gas at the station where he used to work as a kid, talked to the owner, who was still a friend. He used his radar detector against speed traps and flew along the Long Island Expressway before cutting through the city to the Holland Tunnel and driving north. He thought of the cars he passed as fish, hooking them and reeling them in. They never got away.

12

They were on another two-day overnight the weekend Will showed up. Wallace had been giving Alison pointers on rowing the raft and teaching her how to read the river: where the channels were among the rocks, the hydraulics or holes you didn't want to get stuck in, why it was imperative to avoid strainers, downed trees that can trap you underwater. The rafts were nearly indestructible, and rowing one solo, with only equipment, coolers, and dry bags securely strapped down, it was pretty hard to flip it over. She learned fast, and at the end of June he let her do it on the overnight.

She learned how, facing downriver, to use the oars to turn the boat one way or another to slide over and around rocks, to row in reverse to hover and watch, to row forward to pick up a little speed, find a channel, and not get stuck behind a big rock. She was game, patient, and unafraid. No panic, no problem, he'd told her. Then at the campsite by the Cedar River, she nailed the landing, rowing hard to shore. She felt and looked very serious going through the gorge and steep rapids the next day and made it all the way to North River without losing her grip on the oars or her balance in the boat. At the end, he said she was now a genuine river runner, a wild-water rafter, and in somewhat select company. Alison had seldom felt stronger.

She would lose some of that a day later at the general store in Newcomb when Bobby, one of the retired regulars who drank coffee there every morning, stopped her and told her about the fellow in the Mustang.

"The original American muscle car. Of course, this wasn't the 1964 vehicle. It was one of those hatchback jobs. Which I don't think very much of," Bobby said. "They had a very good design at the start. You can see what's wrong with the American automakers. "

She finally cut him off. She already knew the answer to her question. "What guy?"

"He didn't say. Big fella. Don't know exactly how he fit in that little bucket seat. He said he was a friend of yours and wanted to know where to find you. And Lottie too. He went up the road to see if they had a motorboat he could rent. Of course, all they've got are canoes and kayaks. I guess that didn't suit him."

"This was Saturday?"

"Saturday, wasn't it, Rita, when that guy came here looking for Alison?"

"It was Saturday," she said, looking up from frying burgers for a pair of lunch customers.

"That was it?" Alison said. "He didn't stay? Didn't come back? Did he say anything?"

"Just that he was looking for you," Bobby said.

"He did come back," Rita said, moving behind the cash register. "I guess he knew you were working for a rafter out of Lake Placid. I think, Bobby, you told him. And he went up there. And then he came back here 'cause I guess you weren't there."

For a moment, Alison felt she couldn't breathe. She asked more questions, and it was clear he hadn't returned Sunday. Maybe Will figured out they were gone for two days. And clearly he knew where she was staying, where she was working, where she was. Bobby was a talker and no doubt told him everything he knew. She called her mother on the pay phone in the booth outside. They chatted briefly, then Alison impatiently brought up the subject of Will. And it came out that her mother had let it slip. Will had called her, said he was looking for Alison and that he had some things that were hers he wanted to return, but he didn't know where.

"I told him that wouldn't work anyway since you were out there in the woods with your aunt," her mother said. "He asked if there wasn't a general delivery mailbox he could send things to. And I told him that Newcomb doesn't even have a post office so he should just forget it. I knew you didn't want to see him. And I never cared for him. He was beneath you. And I told him so. Right there on the phone."

Alison corrected her about the post office, then hung up on her, got in Lottie's truck, and drove to Lafleur's place. He was out back, rinsing the wetsuits with a hose.

"What's up?" he said, smiling, though she walked up to him agitated.

"There's a problem."

"Really?"

"There's a guy looking for me, and he came around this weekend while we were gone. He also came here, I'm pretty sure. You should check and see if anything's missing or stolen."

"Is that right? Who is this guy?"

"A guy I used to know."

"And what do you think he wants?"

Alison thought about it. "Me."

Wallace handed her a wetsuit and grabbed another. "Help me for a minute, and let's talk."

"What? Are you out of your mind?"

It was a gray day, promising drizzle, maybe a downpour.

"No. This needs to get done. And it would be easier before the rain comes. I'll get the gear inside to hang it up and dry it out. Besides, is he still here?"

"Not that I know of."

"Then we've got time."

Lafleur sounded so certain, so unruffled, that for a moment she felt calmer. They finished rinsing the gear and hanging it up. There wouldn't be another trip again until the weekend, though he said soon they'd be busy almost every day through high summer, running trips one day and cleaning up and restocking the next. He kept his guns locked in a heavy rack, and they were still there. Wallace didn't lock his door, but there was no sign anybody had been inside. It was the Adirondacks. He had never been robbed and didn't expect to be.

He asked her to tell him the story, promising he wouldn't share it without her consent. And so while they worked, Alison described the six-month relationship, Will's sweetness at first and his possessiveness later. She told him about the ripped-out phone, the car chase and near run-in with the police, the harassing phone calls, and how her mother had revealed where Alison had gone. She felt a little better for telling it, but not much.

"Now what?" he said.

"He'll be back."

"And what do you think he'll do?"

"Force me to go," she said. "Hurt me."

"Can he do that?"

"What do you mean, can he do that? What kind of stupid question is that?" She was shouting.

"Do you want a gun?" he asked. "I've got a shotgun that's easy to use. You can keep it with you. It can be pretty persuasive. With one of those in hand, nobody can make you do much of anything. And you can hurt them, if you need to."

"Lottie's got one."

"And knows how to use it, I'll bet." Lafleur laughed. "I'd bet you're a lot safer with her than this guy is."

"I don't know what he'll do. It's not funny. You have no idea what it's like. It's the same as being hunted. You're a hunter, right? What do you think it's like to be on the other end? Have you ever thought about that?"

"Often," he said. "I'll bet you're safe with me as well."

"You don't know him," Alison said. "He keeps a handgun in his truck, under the seat. He's missing a piece of his ear. He's a lot bigger than you are. You don't know him."

"Actually I think I probably do. But that's beside the point. What's his name? Where's he from exactly? What does he look like? What does his vehicle look like? He has two, right? If we're going to be watching for him, we'll see him coming and probably head off any trouble."

"You can't."

"You might be right, Alison. But you have friends here, and I think it's going to be all right."

She told him Will's name, age, and address and described him, his pickup, and the Mustang. Wallace said he still knew somebody with the state who might check to see if he had a felony warrant or prior convictions, which would present one way of dealing with him.

Alison stopped back at the general store before paddling down to the cabin and explained to both Rita and Bobby that the guy with the Mustang was not a friend and if he ever showed up again, please don't tell him anything. Or tell him she went back to Long Island. And let her or Lottie know. They promised, and she canoed down to the cabin, talked to Lottie, and did some target practice with her bow and with Lottie's shotgun.

13

The things that attracted her to Will were the things she tended to fall in love with. He had a certain comfort with his masculinity, and he liked her femaleness. He was interested in everything about her. He seemed to see her clearly, and he was very gentle at first. And he kissed her slowly and thoroughly. But at twenty-six she should have paid more attention to some of the other signs. She wasn't a virgin. And she'd been in love before, for almost two years in the Carolinas when she was scraping by, a college dropout and not ready to get married to a well-mannered Southern boy who wanted her to join the family and make babies. Instead, flat broke, she went home to her mother's house, which was looking shabby three years after the divorce, and returned to school, back again on Long Island.

The first time she saw Will was at a gas station in Huntington, while she was in line at the pumps. She was driving her mother's Lincoln, also starting to show its wear, like the furniture, the gardens, and the landscaping. Will walked over, picked up a squeegee, and cleaned her windshield. Then he walked to the window and asked for her phone number. She was wearing a yellow dress and silver earrings. She laughed at him and said no, she didn't give her number to strangers. He walked back to his pickup truck and left. The next time was in a bar near the university, a dive where Alison and her friends liked to play darts or pool and generally tart around. They were up to no good as usual, flirtatious and bitchy and funny.

Monica turned heads with her blond mane and athletic body; she liked to toss her hair and say, "Will there be anybody more beautiful than me there tonight?" Alison and Teresa would answer, "Not at Joe's," and they would burst out laughing. It was a hole in the wall frequented by construction workers, bikers, students, old-timers, and a soccer team that the owner sponsored. In summer there would be a line out the door. But they never waited. Teresa, short and voluptuous, with long black hair, pale skin, and red lips, would stand in front of the bouncer with her hands folded in prayer, her head bowed, looking like a sexy Virgin Mary, and he always let them in. She had an Italian boyfriend on the soccer team who was jealous of anyone she spoke to and disapproved of Alison and Monica. They'd overdress for the place, were always occupied talking to other men and boys, and they would ignore Naldo. He'd get crazy. That led to screaming matches with Teresa; sometimes they got thrown out, and they'd go back to her apartment, where Teresa said he worshipped her body. And that, her friends replied, was the true calling of a voluptuous virgin.

But one weekend Will was sitting in a booth when Alison walked in. She raised her eyebrows in mock surprise as she passed by and kept walking, then forgot about him. He didn't approach her all night. Later, after Teresa and Monica were already gone, Alison walked out and noticed Will was following her. In the parking lot across the street, he talked to her but kept his distance. She couldn't recall what they said. But it was fall, chilly, with a sharp wind. Alison was cold, and he stepped closer, blocking the wind. So she let him stand closer than she normally would. Then he was right up beside her, and finally in front of her, then against her. She was tall and slender, and as usual wore three-inch heels under her jeans. And he was as tall, with wide shoulders. She felt warm there. And he kissed her and pressed the full length of himself against her until she could feel the button of his jeans and the tension in his back. But Alison was tired and drew away from him.

"Well, I'll see you," she said.

"What's your phone number?"

"You'll never remember it."

"Oh, yes I will."

And he did.

When she saw him again, he asked about his left earlobe. Will told her he lost a piece of it in a bar fight, but after he saw the look on her face he seemed to immediately regret it. She realized later that Joe's wasn't his joint and maybe he'd staked it out waiting for her, without knowing her but intending to. That maybe he saw the student parking sticker in her mother's car and started cruising off-campus hangouts. Perhaps she represented something else to him, which he suspected from the start and would later confirm, that she'd been a rich girl from Cold Spring Harbor whose family lived in a six-bedroom house on eight acres of woods and lawn. She'd tried to hide that, though at the end she'd used it to try to intimidate him and keep him away. It didn't work. And it was hardly true anymore.

Will had bought her many things: a vacuum cleaner, flowers many times, including a crystal vase that she smashed, a ring, a hair clip, a hideous necklace, and a workout tape. When he gave her the tape he told her if she lost some weight she'd have a perfect ass. That night, she left it unopened on a table and cried by herself. At the end of their relationship she cried a lot, so much that even Will realized it might be over.

They weren't arguing anymore at that point, just not enjoying each other's company. By then, he had slept with his old girlfriend, and that took some of the shine off the relationship. She'd actually wanted to forgive him. He asked her to, and it's not like it even mattered that much to her. But on reflection she thought if he was pushing things like that when they'd been living together for six months, what was it going to be like in a year? At some point he'd leave, or disregard her altogether. She began to lose the feeling for him.

And then one Saturday she went to a football game with her friend Rob, another graduate student, and they were just hanging around drinking beer and being friendly. But Rob kept nudging her to get her attention and sat closer than he needed to and put an arm around her to pull her sweater over her shoulder. After the game, walking to her car, he picked her up and swung her around to make some point, and she laughed. It was fun to be with him, a flirtation. But somebody must have seen them and called Will.

When she returned to the house, Will was putting plastic sheeting over the sliding doors to keep the draft out of the kitchen. He was drinking a long-neck beer, and she got a bad feeling as she took her coat off.

"Where have you been?"

"I went to a football game."

"With who?"

"No one."

"Who?"

"Monica. And I saw some other people there."

"I'm going to ask you again. With who?"

"None of your business." She was angry, finally.

He walked over quickly and grabbed her arm. She pulled free and ran into the bedroom and slammed the door. Then it was silent for a long time, and she heard furniture being dragged across the floor. She tried the door. He'd blocked it. She picked up the phone in the bedroom and began to dial, but then she heard a popping sound and the line went dead. He'd ripped the phone wire out of the wall. When she heard furniture sliding again, she locked the door. He got a screwdriver and jimmied the lock. He came in. Alison sat meekly on the bed, thinking it might be the last thing she ever did. She wondered if he had the gun that he kept under the seat of his truck.

"What do you want?" she said quietly.

"I want to talk to you."

"Really? That's all? I thought you were mad at me."

"I am mad. But I have some things I want to say."

He wanted her to listen. So she did. She thought if she played this part right he would calm down. When he was done, she sat for several minutes.

"You must be tired," she said.

"I am."

"Me too. We both need to get some sleep. I can't stay here tonight. I'm going home. "

"You could just stay," he said.

"Probably it's best, just for tonight, so you can have a little space and think about what you really want."

Just before she left in her rusted-out Mazda, he said, "Are you coming back tomorrow?"

"Yes. I'm coming back tomorrow."

"Okay," he said. "We'll work this out."

"Yes. We'll work this out."

She never went back. When he called her house, her mother told him in her sharp way that he was not good enough for Alison. He couldn't get through to talk to her. She found the sublet in the city, sold her car, finished her semester on Long Island, commuting by train if she had to go to campus, and ran into him finally in an upscale Huntington tavern, where he looked out of place. While he was up at the bar buying a beer, she left. He chased her mother's Lincoln all the way into TriBeCa, where he drove off from the cops, but somehow got her phone number at the sublet.

14

When Donny, Wallace, and the band played at the roadhouse in St. Regis Falls, Wallace invited Alison. It was noisy, sweaty, fun, and beer flowed. The statuesque blond fiddler–the only woman in the band–stole the show playing fast bluegrass. Alison surprised herself at being relieved that the fiddler wasn't with Lafleur. It seemed silly to feel a twinge of jealousy. Alison reminded herself she was now a river guide, though she had yet to get a license from the state, and that was more interesting than being a musician.

Sometime after 2 a.m., Wallace drove Alison back to Lake Placid and pulled into the parking lot off Main Street where she had left her aunt's truck. Someone had pulled a subcompact into the small space next to it. He stopped his pickup in the lot and turned off the engine and lights. They both got out. It was dimly lit, despite the storefronts and lampposts out on the street and the occasional head-lights from passing cars. The scent of oncoming summer was in the air.

"I hope you're a good driver," Wallace said. "It looks kind of crowded in there."

"I get your van to North River loaded and unscratched, so I think I can manage this."

"How will you get down to the cabin in the dark?" he asked.

"I left the canoe at the outfitters in Newcomb. I'll canoe down."

"Be careful in the dark," he said.

"I've got a flashlight. And the moon's up. Three quarters tonight. Lots of light."

"You have been paying attention," Wallace said. She stopped by her aunt's truck and turned to face him when he asked her, "I don't suppose there's any chance you'd consider working again Wednesday."

"I don't know. Maybe," she replied, teasing him. "You're paying me, right? When do you need to know?"

"Well, let's see. Tomorrow probably. Otherwise I'll need to find Carol or someone else. You know how enthusiastic she is."

"I'll call you. But if you don't hear from me by Wednesday I'd make other plans."

"And, yes, I will be paying you. The money's the same as last time. Cash if you like. Two dollars a trip. However long or short the day."

"Plus beer?" Alison said. "Or was that just tonight."

"Plus beer." He smiled.

"I'll let you know."

She stood there watching him, waiting to see what he would do.

Without any indication or invitation, he stepped forward and pressed his mouth against hers. He'd warned her he would probably try to kiss her—almost as a joke, between sets, telling her it was only because of the way she laughed. And now that he was kissing her, she didn't react right away. She was still. But her mouth was warm, and after a moment her lips, still closed, seemed to press back. And he stepped away.

"Oh, God," she said softly. He didn't know what that meant.

"Was it bad?"

Instead of answering, she put a hand on the lapel of his flannel shirt, gripping it, and pulling him toward her, and kissed him, longer this time, and gently, briefly, caught his lower lip with her teeth and let it go.

She had perfect teeth, he thought, and it made a perfect moment.

When he stepped back, she said, "I'll let you know."

Paddling home under a sky filled with stars, she decided she still liked men, at least in a general way. The beard, the thick and even callused fingers, the eyebrows that jut over the eyes, even the hair on their legs and torsos, the chiseled calves, the heavy boots that looked big next to her sandals, the T-shirts with the names of businesses on them, their deep voices, the jeans that were too big for her, the oxford shirts that were big and loose, that she liked to slip on. She still liked men in the abstract, anyway, and wondered if it might not be better to leave them there.

15

Lafleur decided not to take the train. It was too slow, and he didn't want to be bound by the timetables of railroad lines, whether he took Amtrak out of Rensselaer or Metro North from Poughkeepsie, then the Long Island Rail Road. He didn't want to take his truck, not wishing to waste gasoline or risk its being noticed. He borrowed a friend's Honda Civic and locked the pistol in the trunk. His carry permit wasn't good in New York City or on Long Island, and there was no point in being the least bit reckless.

Starting early on a Sunday afternoon, he took the Northway south out of the mountains and then the Thruway to the Palisades Parkway, crossed the George Washington Bridge, and eventually got on the Long Island Expressway. It was easy and uncomplicated, and he enjoyed the view while making an effort to keep the vibrational level of his chakras attuned and harmonious for six hours all the way to Hempstead. He sang peaceful songs and in between thought of Alison's voice and spontaneous laughter. It was easy enough to find Will's house, in a small cul-de-sac near the highway and therefore noisy from the traffic and not too desirable. There were three vehicles in the short driveway, a Chevy pickup, a Mustang, and a panel truck with a logo on the side for a plumbing business. Alison said Will always watched the Mets games with his brother George, and they drank a lot of beer and yelled at the television. She once found that charming, very male, and fun. Not anymore.

Since his visit to Newcomb, Will had called the general store twice, leaving messages for Alison about his plans to come up. Alison was so upset that she was thinking about quitting the rafting business and leaving the mountains. She told Wallace about the phone calls. Over the next few days, without telling her, he made up his mind what to do.

He drove past the house, made sure of his route back to the highway, saw his footpath through the yards to the vehicle, and parked in a spot that wasn't clearly visible from any house. He waited for an hour. Then he walked around to the trunk, opened it, checked the full cylinder of the big revolver, felt its heft, and slid it into the large interior pocket of his jacket. He wore a knit hat pulled low on his head. His mustache and beard obscured his face. He reminded himself, as he walked down the street, that he grew up on the streets of Utica and had climbed McKinley and the Matterhorn and come back, that he was the alpha male in every pack that he needed to be in, and there wasn't much he wouldn't do to settle this thing for Alison and protect her if necessary. Then he breathed and let it go.

He went up the front steps of the bungalow, listened to the traffic on the expressway, and thought it would nearly swallow the indoor blast of a .357, which was very loud. If it came to that, the neighbors wouldn't be sure what they heard. And frankly, finally, he didn't care. He rang the doorbell. The guy who answered was as big as Alison had described, more than two hundred pounds and over six feet. About thirty. He had a can of Budweiser in his hand. The television was on, the volume up high, in the room right behind him.

"I didn't order a pizza," Will said, looking at the scruffy stranger in a heavy coat on his front step.

"I didn't bring one," Wallace said. He laughed. "I brought you something from Alison."

Will looked at him more closely. "Who are you?"

"A friend. Can I come in?" Wallace said mildly. "I'll show you what I've got."

Will walked back inside, leaving the door open, and Wallace followed and closed the door. Will sat on an oversize sofa, next to a slightly larger version of himself, but a little more overfed. Cans of beer, chips, and other snack foods were scattered on the coffee table. George had his legs up on the end of it, ankles crossed.

"Can you turn that down a little?" Wallace said. "It's kind of hard to hear."

Will picked up the remote and lowered the volume.

"Who the fuck's this guy?" George said.

It had always been clear to Wallace that as dangerous as someone could be, usually he was worse with his brother around. They egged each other on, set their own boundaries by consensus. He'd learned the hard way that the best guarantee of being attacked from behind was to throw down with a guy's brother, who nine times out of ten would challenge you in the first place because his brother was there. Having somebody clearly on their side made them bolder, irrational. He knew coming into this that would probably be the case, and in a way he wanted to get it all out of the way at once. He was glad George was there.

"What we've got here are Utica rules," Wallace said softly. He unzipped his jacket, reaching slowly inside for the butt of the revolver, sliding it out like a gift. "Nobody moves, and nobody gets hurt."

He held the gun in his right hand, pointing the long barrel upward, and with his left finger pointed at Will and George.

"What the fuck!" George said. He lowered his feet. Will stayed silent, leaning forward. Wallace figured it was a 12-by-12-foot room, which put both men about eight feet from him. It wouldn't be much trouble to get off a couple shots before they could cross the space. And unlike the aggressive mother bear he'd driven off his back deck the previous summer with two loud pistol shots under her feet, he wasn't so sure he wouldn't have to kill these two.

"As you know, Alison lives up north now. And she has friends up there. Me and some others. And so we know when you come up. And we even know when you write letters and make phone calls. We are a peaceful group. But we do not, and I'm telling you this as a friend, we do not allow women in those mountains to be abused."

"What?" Will said, as if he thought this guy was crazy.

"Now wait," Wallace said, still talking softly. "Now, we're against hitting. And we're against threatening. And, we don't allow stalking. That's something you do to wild animals. That's not something you do to people."

"Bullshit!" Will said. He started to stand up.

Wallace turned his left hand palm forward, motioning Will to stop. He pointed the pistol at his chest. Will sat down.

"Let me explain it this way," Wallace said, still speaking softly. "It's very, very simple. She knows where you are. I had no trouble finding you, so I'm sure she can if she wants to. But she doesn't. Do you see that?"

Will didn't say anything.

Wallace repeated himself, pointing the gun at Will's head. "Do you see that?"

"How do you know?"

"Because I do. Now here's the second part. If you ever come up there again, if you ever contact her again, I'll kill you."

"What?" George said. "Are you fucking nuts?"

"Not at all. I'm from the Adirondacks, where we solve things a little differently. So here's what I'm saying. Should I catch you up there, I'm going to shoot you like a deer. And like a deer, I'm going to hang you by your ankles and gut you. And leave your gut pile for the coyotes. And bury the rest of you deep in the woods, where the rangers don't go. That way it's done. It's very old school. But trust me, the mountains have secrets."

"You're out of your fucking mind," George said.

"No, George, I'm not. So protect your brother. Keep him safe. Keep him out of my mountains. I'm a hunter, and it's all the same to me. Today I'm your friend. Tomorrow, I could still be your friend. And Will's friend. But only if he practices kindness toward Alison. If she loves you, Will, she'll find you. But it's her choice, too. Do you see that?"

Will didn't say anything. He stared at Wallace. He didn't look like he was inclined to get up now.

"I can't leave until you tell me you do." Wallace cocked the hammer, pointing the gun at Will's eye, and took a step forward.

"I understand."

"And George, do you see what's at stake here for your brother to do the right thing? Tell me."

George nodded vaguely.

"Good. Alison said you were handsome and rugged, Will. And smart. Clearly she's right."

Wallace gently lowered the hammer. He walked to the door, which wasn't entirely closed. When he pulled it shut behind him, they were still sitting. He put the gun back in his coat and walked quickly around the other side of the house, jogged through the backyard and another yard to the street and along it to his car. He drove down the street, turned twice, turned on his headlights, headed to the highway entrance ramp. He drove on the crowded expressway toward the city, took the bridge back into New Jersey, and then rode the Palisades north.

He got out at the first overlook, took in the vista of the city, and put the pistol away again in the trunk. It had served him well. It usually hung at night from the wall, out of sight but within easy reach by his bed. But right now it was just a tool, and he took no particular pleasure in having it rest against his chest. He worked on the vibration of his chakras the rest of the way home.

16

A few weeks later, Wallace drove Alison north on Route 73, through Keene Valley among the High Peaks and past little Chapel Pond. He pointed out some climbers on the cliffs overlooking the water. Soon after he turned onto a narrow road through the woods that led to the Ausable Club, a fine monument to the days when Wasps ruled the world. The caterers had set up long tables draped with white linen on the wide, gently sloping lawn. Most were under canvas pavilions put up for the event, also white. It was sunny with no breeze and only a few scattered clouds in the sky. Alison jumped out of the truck and ran up to the cottages to find the wedding party. The bride-to-be, an old friend Alison had recently seen in Lake Placid by accident, and her other bridesmaids had taken over a series of rooms in one building, where they were drinking champagne. They shrieked when she walked in. Wallace talked to some of the catering staff he knew, then got out of their way, lying in the sunshine near the bottom of the lawn, shielded from view by the last table, chewing on a piece of grass and watching a large cumulus cloud drift from the west. Alison, barefoot and wearing her bridesmaid's dress, her hair loosely pinned up and no makeup, found him there. She carried a pair of overfilled champagne flutes, wine spilling over the fingers of her right hand as she sipped from the glass in her left.

"You look relaxed," she said.

"I figured down here, nobody will ask me to leave. They can't even see me from the golf course. Mistake me for the caddie who ran away twenty years ago and was never seen again."

"Don't get too comfortable," she said. "You've got to get changed and come back."

"Well, you know, this really isn't my kind of affair."

"It's too late now, buster. I brought you champagne."

She set the glasses on the grass and sat down next to him, carefully hiking her red and white floral-print dress. She handed him a flute. He set it down, took the tail of his shirt, and dried her right hand.

"Thank you," he said.

"You're always thanking me. I hate it when you say that."

"Why?"

"It's what you'd say to a stranger."

"Just trying to be polite," he said, and sipped. "Good champagne. Thank you."

"If you're polite again, I'll have to punish you." She drank. "Don't test me."

"You know what I'll say then?" Wallace slowly drained his glass. He leaned closer and touched her shoulder where it was exposed above the low neckline. "That you have flawless skin on your shoulder. And then, thank you, sir, may I have another."

"That's it." Alison emptied her glass and laid it next to his. "You're done." She pushed him back, half under the tablecloth, and he laughed.

"You'll stain your dress. And your reputation."

She hiked it up and knelt over him.

"Seriously. You should take it off, so you don't damage it, and come under here where I can see if you're flawless everywhere." He shifted his hips under the table, then his back, taking her with him. "Watch your head."

It was cool there and smelled like the grass. And it was suddenly quiet, and private. She leaned close and kissed him, brushing his lips, still damp with champagne. A fragment of sunshine cast light under the edge of the tablecloth, and in the deep shade she leaned back again and saw him smiling.

"Your beard is kind of rough," she said. He'd been on the river every other day and hadn't shaved the stubble in a week. He'd shaved his beard off recently, just before the day he went out of town. His black hair was curly and damp from the shower. "But I kind of like it."

She rubbed her cheek against the dark stubble. They'd held hands twice that week, briefly. And since the parking lot, she'd kissed him once lightly apropos of nothing. Whatever the connection was, it felt effortless and mildly electric to her. Wallace reached up and opened the clip that held her hair up behind her head.

"Oh," she said, softly. It fell around their faces. She turned her head and found his mouth again and kissed him slowly and for a long time.

"You've been cast under my spell," Alison said. He wrapped his arms around her and held her against him. He kissed her mouth, then her throat. He lay his head back, listening, and waiting.

"I have to go," she said.

"You do."

"I have to go."

She piled her hair up and clipped it more or less behind her head again. Wallace lifted the edge of the tablecloth and looked out at the lower lawn.

"I think it's clear," he said, laughing again. "There's nobody there."

She kissed him quickly, ducked under the tablecloth, gathered the two champagne flutes, and walked around the table and up the lawn, past the waitresses and waiters, who seemed too busy to pay much attention.

Wallace rolled out from under the white linen, stood up slowly, and walked down to the truck. Only when he reached it did he look back, but she had already gone inside.

17

Alison and the other four bridesmaids created a stunning backdrop, like exotic red-and-white birds in the green landscape, complementing the bride. Claudette wore a tight-waisted gown off the shoulders, with her blond hair in a French braid. Their white stiletto sandals lasted the length of the outdoor ceremony and formal photographs.

"You look fabulous," Alison said, unsurprised. Her childhood friend had had exquisite taste in clothes and in her bedroom decor when they were growing up in Cold Spring Harbor.

"It feels providential that you're here," Claudette said. "Is the dress all right?"

"Fine. Maybe a little short. But as a late substitution, it's surprisingly good. I think my friend will appreciate it."

"I don't think he's the only one," Claudette said. "Jim is actually a catch, in case you didn't notice. And he's noticing you. After the rehearsal dinner he asked John who exactly you were. And look at him now. He cleans up very well. That's why I put you with him. He's a bond trader with John."

"I don't know. There may be time for bond traders later. "

"John and Jim are going to do well. Just in case you wondered. Remember as little girls when we used to plan our weddings?"

"I think," Alison said, "you outdid yourself."

Standing in the reception line, all the bridesmaids were barefoot, as was Claudette. The groomsmen wore black tuxes, though it was an afternoon wedding in July and they appeared to be sweating. As soon as the guests passed through the receiving line the men undid their bow ties, shed their jackets, rolled up their sleeves, and began hitting the cold champagne and chilled Mexican beer to cool off. About two hundred people milled around the two bars on the lawn or gathered near the string quartet, which had played Pachelbel's Canon for the procession and created a soft background of Vivaldi after the vows. Waitresses in black pants, crisp white shirts, and black sneakers brought champagne around and silver trays of hors d'oeuvres.

Wallace knew most of them. They worked for Susan's new catering company out of the country club, and he made it a point to say hello to each one.

"Are you friends with the bride or groom?" Carol asked sarcastically, pouring him a Coke at the bar.

"Neither, actually," Wallace said, leaning in and speaking softly.

"Are you crashing the reception?"

"Can you keep a secret?"

"Sure."

"I'm with one of the bridesmaids."

"Really?" Carol looked over the lawn, noting those she could see. Three were in a group. Another was bookended by two groomsmen, laughing.

"The tall one."

"Her? Isn't it enough that she's working for you now?" Carol shook her head, frowning. "You always did have a way with the help. She seems to be having some fun. And not with you."

"You know, Carol, it's not about me," Wallace said, intending to sound ironic. "It's about how she feels. And I'd say that she feels good."

"How long has this been going on?"

"I'd say it started about an hour ago."

"Funny. Not the reception. This thing with the bridesmaid."

"She's been working for me this summer off and on, as you know, and she asked me to escort her. Apparently she knew the bride from long ago. She ran into her in Lake Placid, and one of the regular bridesmaids couldn't make it at the last minute. And besides, this way I get to talk to you."

"Flattery will get you nowhere. And she doesn't really look like she needs an escort."

"You're absolutely right about that. So I think I'll just circulate a little here among my people." He gestured over the crowd, mostly well-heeled New Yorkers, the women in tailored dresses and jewels, the men in summer-weight suits. Wallace shot the cuffs on his black linen sportcoat, which he wore over a pressed white shirt open at the neck, checked the crease in his new jeans, and rubbed the top of each shiny cowboy boot against the back of the other leg. "But give me one for the road first."

Carol poured him another Coke. Within the hour she phoned Susan, who was also her friend. She was coming by anyway to check on things, but she would arrive sooner than planned.

Alison and the rest of the bridal party sat together for dinner and toasts, and Jim kept the conversation going in a jocular way, but smart.

"Are you good as a bond trader?" she asked.

"I'm all right," he said.

"What does it take?"

"Clients. Money. Naked aggression." He laughed. It was both a joke and sincere.

She scanned the crowd for Wallace, who had waved to her once when he arrived, then disappeared during dinner. She found him afterward helping the band set up and test its microphones and speakers near the main building.

"Alison, you know Donny," Wallace said. "It's his band tonight."

He looked like a stockier version of Wallace, with lighter hair and a short reddish beard.

"Charmed again," Donny said, and held her hand in both of his, for too long, as if they'd just met and he couldn't get over it.

"Sometimes, you know, Donny rows my second raft. Like you, only he's not nearly as attractive. You are spectacular."

"And sometimes," Donny said, "Wallace plays in my band."

"Sometimes?" Alison said, pulling her hand back finally.

"When we're together, with everybody else, like at the roadhouse, we call the band Mostly Willing, right? When it's just Donny and assorted friends, we call it Half Willing." Wallace laughed.

"Then you'd better plan on sitting in," Donny said. "I can't believe you'd give up a gig to be a wedding guest. What's happened to you?"

When the equipment was set up, floodlights illuminated the upper lawn, and torches were lit around the perimeter to deter the mosquitoes, which were gathering at dusk. Guided by Claudette's father, Donny made a few announcements, then they began playing a slow country waltz for the couple, followed by the elegiac "Ashokan Farewell" for the father and daughter. Wilhelmina, who'd been a serious music student at Potsdam and played seven instruments, was haunting and pitch perfect with her violin. The musicians segued next into a soft, then louder version of "Kansas City," which they were playing when Susan arrived. The wedding party swarmed onto the grass in front of the band and started dancing. Alison didn't notice, until the third or fourth song, the woman who was bending Wallace's ear in the shadows, smiling, standing close, touching his sleeve.

The liquor was pouring, torches were flickering, and the crowd was getting more boisterous when the musicians slowed things down with "I Will Always Love You," Dolly Parton's anthem about permanent and passing love. Jim asked Alison to dance, and she accepted. He held her close. She noticed Wallace had taken a place near the back of the musicians, and he waved as she swayed past.

"Your Cheatin' Heart" followed, and Lafleur pulled a harmonica out of his shirt pocket and played riffs over the top, sharing the tall blonde's microphone. He and Donny laughed, like they didn't have a care in the world and never would.

In a cranked-up version of "Don't Think Twice, It's All Right," Wallace sounded like an older Dylan with a gravelly voice. "Goodbye is too good a word, babe, so I'll just say fare thee well." She caught his eye in that moment, standing with her arm around Claudette, who was explaining to her something about the Italian sun coast in July, where she and her new husband were going. Wallace shook his head and winked.

"How do we do it?" he said into the microphone afterward.

They did a cover of "The Weight" and took a break.

Alison found him at the bar.

"You are still the most beautiful woman here. Though I don't feel sorry at all for the bride. She is something."

"Thank you," Alison said, "You and your friends really are good musicians. I guess I was too busy having fun the other night to pay close attention."

"Donny is a musician. Wilhelmina, she is for sure. The other guys, too. I just drop some stuff in behind."

"I liked it."

"Well, thank you." He got a long-neck beer from Carol and formally introduced Alison again, who took another glass of champagne and nodded coolly. "You two met briefly, but I think you're ready to like each other now," he said.

"I think Susan's still here," Carol said.

"Was that the woman you were talking to?"

"Right," Wallace said.

"What was that about?" Alison said.

"She thinks we should get back together."

"And what did you tell her?"

"Well, I told her the job side of things has been filled, at least for a little while. She ran the business and did it pretty well."

"And what about the rest of it?"

"I guess," Wallace said, "that you'll let me know."

Alison kissed him lightly on the mouth and walked back into the crowd. She chatted and laughed and flirted the rest of the night. Wallace played the entire second set on conga drums. When the band was packing up, she asked him for a ride home.

18

Alison changed into jeans and a T-shirt. She left the bridesmaid's dress for Claudette's friend who'd missed the wedding. It was hers, after all, and Alison had made up her mind when she left the city not to collect anything for a while. The mountains didn't mean that to her. What she wanted to take back, when this was over, was the sense of well-being that had sustained her throughout her teens after her last Adirondack summer. Watching Wallace tonight convinced her. This place was time out of mind, a place to be something else, somebody else. She almost went off with Jim for the night, she had been that angry. It was a reflexive move from her salad days. Funny how easy guys were, if you just wanted to get their attention, and how treacherous they were, once you had it. Bastards. She thought about Will, an utter shit, and wondered if Jim was a real prospect or just a good time at a wedding, and goddamn Wallace and his casual indifference. Then she thought about Lottie and wondered who needs any of these men. She decided the safest thing was to return to Newcomb tonight and reconsider how much she needed the money and whether she wanted to keep working for Wallace the rest of the summer.

Alison walked in the dark along the club road to the lower parking lot. The bride and groom were long gone. Most of those in the wedding party had hiked to Lower Ausable Lake to skinny-dip. She resisted serious pressure to join them. As she approached the parking lot, she heard two men talking and recognized Wallace's low voice. Coming closer, she took a deep breath of sweet scented air and said, "Hey."

"Ready to go?"

"Yes."

They said goodnight to Donny, who again took her hand too long. When she got in the truck, she pulled the door closed hard and stared out the window. Wallace drove across the gravel lot and to the highway.

"Where are we going?" he asked.

"Newcomb."

"Right." He turned onto Route 73 and drove toward the Northway.

They remained silent during the ten miles down the winding two-lane. They left the windows open, bringing soft, heavy air and the smell of balsam and pine into the cab. Only a few cars passed the other way.

"Is everything all right?" he asked when they slowed for the turn onto the superhighway.

"Yes. Why?"

"You've been quiet."

"It's just that I'm so sick of these games. I thought it was different here."

"What games? I don't get it," Wallace said.

"What were you doing hanging around with your old girlfriend?"

"I wasn't."

"I saw you. You practically had your arms around her. And she wants to get back together. Well, good for you. But you know what really pisses me off? You couldn't even bother to say hello."

"Whoa, darlin', if that's what's wrong, I'm very sorry. I didn't say hello because you were busy, and it looked like you were having fun. New friends. I don't know. Did wave, though. I'm your friend, too, but I don't feel like I actually have any claim on you."

They continued on in silence for a while.

"I wouldn't mind if I did, but it's not up to me," Wallace said, choosing his words slowly. "And as far as Susan goes, I'm not getting back with her. The last time I saw her, it was just before I climbed out a window. There were some things to talk about. I'm sorry, but I'm not going to pretend I don't know her. That would be wrong."

"You climbed out a window?"

Lafleur described his parting from Susan while they headed down the exit ramp and onto the two-lane to Newcomb.

"That's so juvenile," Alison said.

"What was?"

"Climbing out the window. How old are you, ten?"

"In some ways, that could be. But it wasn't going to be any better if I went back through that door and felt I had to restrain her. That would have been humiliating for both of us."

"As opposed to sneaking away?"

"She said she figured out within five minutes that I was gone. And she's intact. Pretty good, I think."

"Then why does she want to get back together with you?" Alison said.

"That's a really good question. She still thinks she can change me, I guess. But I believe less so than before. And I'll bet you that within a year she'll find somebody who looks at the world the same way she does. There are a lot more guys up here than women, in case you didn't notice. Of course," Wallace added, and laughed, "he probably won't ... never mind."

"Probably won't what?"

"It's not important. And it would be a mistake to talk about, at the moment."

She got quiet again, and they rode down the rest of the way to Newcomb in silence. He parked in the outfitter's driveway and helped Alison carry the canoe, which was behind the building, down to the water.

"I booked another trip in August," Lafleur said. "It's a big group. Do you want to guide the second raft with paddlers in it?"

"Do you think I'm ready?" Alison asked.

"Yes, I do. You will be."

Alison put one life vest on the bottom of the canoe to kneel on and laid a paddle next to it. She put on the other vest, clipped her backpack to the front thwart, and set the flashlight where it would be within reach. The river glistened in the moonlight.

"What I was going to say before, not that it matters at all, is that whatever guy Susan finds, he probably won't not argue with her. But that's irrelevant, and I won't bring her up again," Wallace said. "It was not my intention to upset you, and I apologize. I wanted to say hello, but it looked like you were where you belonged and wanted to be. And I'm easy to find."

The thing that Alison picked up on initially was the last thing he said. She wanted to say, sarcastically, "You are easy," but for the first time in a while she let the sharp remark die on her tongue.

She pushed the Grumman into the water and started paddling downstream. Wallace listened to the crickets and watched. He hadn't expected to feel this way, and he sensed it would not be the last time they said goodbye.

19

They had some free days the following week, and after watching how well Alison had handled the cargo raft and her aunt's Grumman, Wallace suggested they try the two-day whitewater trip in a canoe. It was a different experience in a small boat, he said, requiring a deeper and more intimate understanding of the river. It was also more dangerous. He proposed they put in early on the second day, ahead of the bubble and the rafts. It would be somewhat scratchier at first, and they'd have to wear helmets, even him. He could borrow a friend's plastic canoe, one that could take a beating.

"A helmet for you?" Alison said. "That's not much for, you know, macho outdoorsman style."

"Even me. It's all about the river, and what she demands she demands."

"So the river's a she."

"Certainly."

He came down the evening before to the cabin to assure Lottie that they'd be safe. She gave her approval only reluctantly, after calling them fools. "What did you buy those big expensive rafts for if you're not going to use them?" she asked.

Lafleur paddled back up to Newcomb, drove home, packed, slept, and was back with the loaded canoe by 8 a.m. One of waterproof bags held their clothes, two sleeping bags, and a tarp. The other had food and water bottles. Wallace always drank from the fast-running Hudson near the Cedar confluence and planned to refill the bottles there. He also brought two bottles of wine, wrapped in his clothing. Both bags lay in the middle of the canoe, clipped to the thwarts. He had Alison kneel in the bow, on an extra life vest, and instructed her when to reach down and pry the water with her paddle, to push the bow away from something, when to reach out and draw, or pull the bow in that direction, and when to brace, laying the paddle across the gunwales to help prevent tipping.

"What about paddling forward?" Alison asked.

"Mostly you won't need to. The river will move us along. Your job is to see the openings and keep the bow pointed downstream. I'll try to keep us in the best channel generally, but you're also going to see submerged rocks and deadheads that the raft would just slide over but we should probably avoid."

"And why are we doing this?"

"Because there's nothing else quite like it. It's the old way. And you will be washed clean by the experience and born new at its terminus."

"You should have been a priest."

As they pushed off in the water, Lottie yelled at them again for being fools. "But goddamn it, come back live fools. Am I understood?"

"Yes ma'am. Maybe Alison should stay and you should come, Lottie."

"Not on your life."

After the flatwater near the cabin, they easily rode the rills where the river ran a little faster. At the first meaningful whitewater, they nearly fell out when the canoe got hung up sideways against a boulder. Lafleur told her to lean downstream to keep the boat from swamping; eventually, he nudged them free. Alison began to feel calmer and asked her question.

She had gone up to Newcomb in the outboard the evening before and phoned her mother, who said she'd received a strange phone call last week from Will about some man with a gun from the Adirondacks that Alison sent to kill him, and he said he was calling the police or something. He was very upset and threatening lawyers and carrying on, and finally Dolores told him again he wasn't worthy of her daughter, who wouldn't stoop to such a low-class thing. Of course, she allowed that her daughter did have a streak that could be cold and vindictive, which Dolores said she herself knew only too well.

"So what do you make of that?" Alison said, turning to look back at him.

"Are you cold to your mother?"

"That's not what I'm talking about. Did you threaten him?"

"Well, I might have explained some things."

"Goddamn you. Who do you think you are? You have no right to do this. Who said you could? And you weren't even going to tell me?" She hit the gunwale with the side of her paddle. "Now what? What happens when he comes looking the next time and takes it out on me because you threatened him?"

Wallace was using his paddle as a rudder, looking downstream. They were starting to move pretty quickly again. "I don't think that's going to happen."

"And how would you know?"

"They seemed to listen to reason."

"Who's they?"

"There were two of them. One was a little bigger and a little uglier. I'm guessing that was his brother. Or else you have really bad taste in men. Not just kind of bad taste."

"You son of a bitch." She smacked the canoe with the paddle. She faced forward, then turned back. "When and where did you do this? Tell me everything that happened."

Lafleur did, leaving nothing out. She cursed him a few more times at intervals. When they got hung up on another large rock, which turned the canoe broadside again, neither saw it coming. The boat tilted and water from upstream quickly started coming in, first as a trickle, then filling the canoe, and they fell out. The river was only waist deep, and Alison waded to shore, using her plastic paddle for balance. Wallace stayed in the fast-flowing water and pushed the canoe farther up the rock, until he could tilt it and pour the water out. He then waded with the canoe to shore, about thirty yards downstream from Alison, who sat shivering under a cedar tree. It was overcast, only in the sixties, and her T-shirt and shorts were soaked. After a while, she walked along the bank to the boat.

"You kind of have to watch the river," Wallace said. "Or else it can get away from you. Are you all right?"

"You kind of have to mind your own goddamn business. And yes, I'm all right. I need to keep moving. I'm cold."

They emptied the rest of the water from the canoe, made sure the bags were still secure and the hull wasn't damaged, and kept paddling.

"I'm pretty sure you won't see him again unless you want to," Wallace said. "I think he believed I'd have shot him dead. I think he still believes it."

"Would you?"

He didn't answer.

"So tell me," Alison said, "what did Will and that asshole brother look like when they were all surprised like that?"

"Well, their eyes did get kind of big. I mean, they thought I was the pizza guy or something. Then the Colt's pretty persuasive. It looks kind of like a cannon. But I was polite. I think the thing that made the biggest impression was the part about being strung up and gutted. About then, I don't think they were even breathing."

Alison let out a whoop of laughter. "My God. That jerk George used to come around to watch baseball, and he'd tell Will to tell me to get him a beer or cook something."

"Did you?"

"What, are you kidding me? Back in the beginning. But not later. I'd leave the room when he came over."

"Do you really think he called the cops?"

"Are you kidding? He's a stalker. Stalkers don't call the cops. Though I suppose if he thought he could get away with it, he would."

They managed the other rapids without trouble. When a northwest wind came along, though, Alison got cold and started to shiver. Then she got splashed and got colder.

"How much farther to the campsite?"

"About a half-hour. You remember this stretch. Why don't you paddle a little more? That will warm you up."

By the time they reached the Cedar, Alison's lips were blue and she was shaking. She could hardly feel her hands. They pulled the canoe up the sandy bank and removed the two big bags.

"I think we need to warm you right away," Wallace said. "Can you feel your fingers?"

"No."

He laid the tarp down and unrolled one of the sleeping bags. He removed Alison's helmet and her Teva sandals, then stripped off her vest, T-shirt, bra, shorts, and panties and rubbed her dry with a nubby towel. He unzipped his sleeping bag, she lay down in it, and he zipped it up again.

"Is that any better?"

"A little." She was still shivering.

Lafleur stripped, toweled off, and slid into the sleeping bag, his chest against Alison's back, his legs against hers, his arms around her, his head resting above and against hers. She shook harder.

"It'll be okay," he said. "It just takes a minute. Your body is the best furnace in the wilderness, that and your friend's body."

She shivered almost constantly for ten minutes and off and on for another twenty. Gradually, their body heat filled the sleeping bag and warmed them through. Alison didn't want to move. After another half-hour, she realized she was sweating against him. She inched around and put her arms around him and entwined their legs.

"Probably we shouldn't do this," he said. "Not now. It's not right. You were hypothermic. You're not thinking clearly."

"I'm not thinking at all," she said. "Are you rejecting me?"

"Of course not."

"Then please shut up. Don't talk. Don't say a word."

She got on top of him, spread her knees outside his, and with no effort at all he was inside her. Neither moved, except to breathe. Later, she couldn't recollect how much time had passed before she lifted her head, closed her mouth on his, and began the slow, gentle rhythm. For a long while, they continued kissing. It ended with the best orgasm she ever had. Certainly the longest, and the slowest.

20

The music of rushing water at the rivers' confluence, which lulled Alison as she drifted off to sleep, took on another quality in the light of day. It was still enveloping, and she could smell the spray of the whitewater, but instead of peaceful, now it seemed cheerful, vibrant. She had slept lying on Lafleur in the sleeping bag, though he got up once to spread the tarp and pull the bag with her inside it more squarely onto the waterproof groundcover. They each got up once to pee, walking off barefoot and naked in the dark among the trees. Sometime in the night they unzipped the bag, which made it a little cooler and created some space to stretch out. She didn't move off him, though, and nestled her head in the space next to his.

They woke late, the sun nearly cresting the trees across the Hudson. She recalled the sunshine on the train ride north, far down the river where it was wide, flat, moving imperceptibly with the tide. This was another world. She didn't think she'd ever want to go back there.

"I'm hungry," Alison said.

"I'll bet you are." Wallace kissed the top of her head softly, then sat up slowly, bringing her with him. "What would you like?"

"Food. A lot of food." She yawned and stretched as he inched sideways and laid her down gently in the soft bag. "You know, comestibles."

"You stay right there, darlin'. And I'll bring you lots of food."

Alison listened while Wallace pulled on his clothes, unpacked the supply bag, and gathered deadwood and kindling for a fire, but then she dozed until he was squatting next to her in his jeans with a steaming mug of coffee.

"How do you like it? I've got sugar, and milk, and some English break-fast tea if you don't like any of those possibilities."

She sat up and wrapped the sleeping bag around her and looked at him.

"I like to see you trying so hard with me," she said. "I've seen you do it with the clients, but this is special."

"You know, Lafleur Whitewater Expeditions aims to please. And you, you are unique. So it's milk and a little sugar, right?"

"You've been paying attention." She took the mug, which already had both in it, and sipped and smiled.

"I've been paying very close attention."

"You can confuse a girl that way."

"Damn. Because all I'm trying to do is clarify things." He looked at her for a moment. "No pressure, though. None whatsoever."

"That's good. Because although I do well with pressure, for the most part, I don't like it." She examined him awhile, then deliberately frowned. "And I don't like rejection."

"No. Of course you don't." He sighed. "And how unlikely."

"You know, everything I've really wanted I've gotten," she said. "I wasn't sure with you, though."

He brought her an omelet, which he'd cooked over the fire in a skillet with diced green peppers and cheddar cheese, as well as raisin toast, sliced oranges and pears, and more coffee. She had two helpings, never leaving the sleeping bag, which draped around her as she ate. She didn't worry that she was half exposed. It felt perfectly natural, and he seemed to feel the same. Alison curled up again while Wallace cleaned up and repacked the canoe, except for the bag with her clothes. Reluctantly, she roused. She stretched, brushed her teeth without getting up, and dressed slowly, feeling like she wanted to capture time, slow it down as much as she could.

"I guess we should go," she said finally.

"If you believe that life can be a succession of perfect moments," he said, "there are more just ahead."

"I'll tell you what I believe," Alison said, putting her damp clothes in a plastic bag and stuffing that into the larger bag, which she buckled closed to make it watertight. "I believe the universe is knowable. It can be known by mankind through the slow process of the scientific method."

"Thank you, professor. I believe that, too. I also believe that you can know it right now, by simply being present to it. You know it. You've always known it. You always will know it. If you allow it."

"That's the child in you."

"Yes. That is the child in me. In all of us. Where it's eternal summer with the perpetual exquisite promise of this perfect moment."

"Your business depends on it."

"More than that. My life depends on it. But enough about me. I'm more interested in you. Show me the world through the eyes of a psychologist."

"Cognitive dissonance explains most everything, and psychodynamic theory explains the rest."

"What is that? You lost me."

"I knew I would," she said. "Okay, it's thinking you understand every motive behind what you do."

"And do you? Do you ever surprise yourself?"

"Lately, quite a lot. I mean, really. Look at this. Who'd have thought it? Not a lot of self-reflection of late. No analysis at all." She was smiling, and Wallace didn't say anything else.

About an hour later, downstream near Indian Falls, Wallace told Alison the story he liked to repeat when he had a raft full of adults.

"That's Virgin Falls," he said, pointing toward the forest. "That's what it's called by the people who know."

"And why is that?" She twisted around in the front of the canoe to see him.

"What they say is that if you pass under the falls, you will be washed pure and a virgin again." Lafleur paddled gently on the right, angling the canoe toward the shore where they could see the narrow falls up under the trees.

"And you know this works, how?"

"So what you can do here is start again. You can undo anywhere you've been, any lover you didn't mean, and you can start over again."

"What if I don't want to?" she said.

"Then you can have the great pleasure of becoming innocent but wise and making love again as if for the first time."

They pulled the canoe onshore, took off their clothes by the side of the waterfall, and walked through holding hands. It was cold. Alison shrieked. On the other side they slid against each other and kissed.

"This is your chance to undo it now if you want to," he said, holding her close. "Later it will be more difficult."

"Do you want to undo this?" There was an edge in her voice.

"No." He studied her face, which he'd been doing all morning, and tried to remember the last time he'd done that with anyone else.

"When I saw you at the wedding I felt sad for the bride. How can she compare? You were perfect in that dress, laughing, barefoot, a strand of hair falling across your neck. And you're more beautiful without it. How do you do that?"

"You've been cast deeply under my spell," Alison said. She motioned him to lie in a bed of soft ferns and lay on him, kissing him again, with more urgency, her fingers buried in his hair. He put his hands against her lower back and held her belly against his. She made a sound in her throat.

"Wait," he said.

"For what?"

"So I can see you just a little."

He rolled to his side, and ran his fingers lightly down her shoulder and arm, across her ribs, and down her hip.

"Your breasts are perfect."

"They're small"

"They're perfect." He looked lower. "And the rest of you."

He pushed her gently to her back. He kissed her mouth, then her throat and one breast. He lay his head on her chest, listening to her heart, then on her belly for a moment, his ear just above her navel, then slid farther. He kissed her belly, hips, and the top of her thighs and lingered high in between, pressing his mouth gently, and with nearly imperceptible movements of his tongue. Alison sighed. She smelled the forest and looked at the trees and the sky and listened to the waterfall. After a while her hips began to move in a way she was distantly aware of. Her hands stretched down into his curls and pulled him harder against her, let him go and pulled again. Her hips rose and fell, and her head turned sharply to the side. He didn't change his rhythm as she pressed against him. After a while, after three short gasps, Alison shuddered and pushed his head away. She lay back, closed her eyes, and drifted on the sensation that ran up her spine and spread everywhere. He lay his head softly on her belly again.

"Do we have to go?" she said.

"Not yet."

After a time, the flotilla of crowded colorful rafts riding the dam release began to appear. They got dressed and followed them down the river.

21

They deliberately took their time getting back on the water, waiting for the last of the rafts to pass. All were commercial outfitters, full of noisy customers with life vests, helmets, and paddles. Lafleur had postponed a booking to the next day so he and Alison could take their trip. He made about three-fourths of his yearly income in summer with rafting. With all the packing, resupplying, and booking, he typically worked every day from late June until early September. It had taken some effort to clear two days for a personal outing, and he couldn't think of a better reason for doing it.

He knew most of the other companies and was friends with several of the guides, though as usual some were new this year, not much more than kids. He didn't know how well they controlled their boats and didn't want to be immediately downstream of any of them, particularly if the canoe got hung up or he and Alison capsized and wound up swimming. He'd planned to stay far ahead of them. However, they couldn't lag far behind now since they needed the extra water from the dam release to get cleanly through some of the shallows that followed the big rapids, especially in the mile before the takeout. They stopped just above the base of a tall limestone cliff called Blue Ledge, where Wallace asked Alison to keep the canoe steady. He rummaged in his bag and pulled out a wooden flute. She looked at him quizzically.

"I'm going to play something in honor of the cliffs and the river and you," he explained.

Alison thought it would be corny and strange and forced herself not to say anything sarcastic. He held the flute to his mouth and slowly produced long, deep, haunting notes that reverberated off the towering rock wall. The music seemed in harmony with the flow of the river. It made her think of Buddhists and meditation, and she wished he'd continue.

"Very Eastern."

"Well, that's good. Because we're about to hit the serious whitewater from here. That was a little gift to the river gods. And I call what's next tai chi on the Hudson."

"We've done this several times this year," Alison said. "It's the same river."

"Not in a small boat," he replied.

"You know, Lewis, when we ran the Cahulawasee down there in the New South, there was an albino boy played the banjo. I guess that weren't so lucky," Alison said, teasing him. She knew he'd read *Deliverance*. It was on his shelf.

She laughed.

"Seriously," Wallace said. He dug in the bag for the helmets and put one on, checked hers, and checked that her safety vest was tight and wouldn't slide up. "It's going to buck differently. Harder. Closer to the rocks. Stay low, keep the bow pointing forward, and I'll try to keep us in the best channel and out of the hydraulics. Any place you see water dropping hard and deep over a big rock, we don't want to be there. Use your pry and draw to avoid the smaller oncoming rocks, too, and we'll keep going downriver. Remember to brace with your paddle across the gunwales on the big drops, but keep your weight low at your knees and butt. And if you swim, don't stand up. Keep your paddle and lie back with your feet up against oncoming rocks and ride it. Swim over to shore in the flat water. Don't worry about the canoe. I'll take care of that."

"Yes, Lewis," she replied, still playing against his concern. She wanted to get going. "This is exactly what you said yesterday. "

"Some things bear repeating."

He was beginning to wonder whether this was a good idea. He hadn't canoed the gorge in a few years, and her entire experience with whitewater canoeing had come in the previous twenty-four hours, and they'd capsized in a much easier stretch. He suggested they take out on the sand beach a hundred yards downstream and portage the canoe the mile and a half up the hiking trail to Minerva. They could call Donny and tell him to pick them up there, instead.

"What, are you kidding me? I didn't come all this way to quit now." Alison wasn't worried. She wasn't afraid of the surf off Fire Island, having played in it since she was a girl, and having been thoroughly thrashed in it and always come back up. She'd been a beach lifeguard one summer for the

National Park Service, though she never had to pull anyone out of the deep water except in training. "If we swim, we swim. I'll rescue you, Lewis. Don't be afraid."

Her teasing and resolve made him feel better, though he still had an uneasy foreboding. He wondered if it was just him feeling off balance from the previous twenty-four hours. He didn't want to say anything to make her overly anxious, which would guarantee mishaps. "I don't really want to lose you now," he said.

"Then tell me you love me, darling, and we can proceed. Or pray for deliverance."

She began paddling, heading them toward the rapids, before he could answer.

They ran the gorge and the narrows beyond, slicing through the chutes between rocks. Wallace kept them in the channels and away from surprise drops. Several other rapids followed in quick succession. At times they hit waves that washed over the gunwales. Alison shrieked and kept getting soaked. It became clear why he had her kneel low and had put inflated rubber bags in the front and rear of the canoe to improve flotation. She strained hard as the canoe tilted and dropped like a plummeting roller-coaster. She pushed off sideways a few times to edge away from onrushing rocks and paddled forward in the slower stretches. She didn't get cold and felt the bright sunshine in between bursts of adrenaline. Lafleur called out the names of the rapids as they passed through them. He bailed water with an old bleach bottle, its top cut off, in the flat water. She liked the name Big Nasty the best. They began to see the rafts ahead and were within fifty yards of the last one when they reached Bus Stop.

A handful of rafts had halted just below, and one was trying to make its way back upstream, the guide in the back calling out paddling instructions. On the right, where a tree had fallen into the river, its roots still attached to the bank, they could see something colorful as they hit the first big drop. In the raft coming slowly upstream, someone in front heaved the throw bag, and its rope snagged in the downed tree. Alison, making small quick strokes to keep the canoe pointed straight, thought she heard somebody yell, "Grab the rope."

"There's a swimmer in that strainer," Lafleur said. "Paddle left, hard."

They both paddled on the left and moved across the river at about a thirty-degree angle and almost immediately lost control of the boat. Then the big hydraulic began to suck the bow toward it.

"Paddle right, hard!" Lafleur shouted, but Alison was already doing that, pushing water sideways. He sunk his paddle deep on the right to move them forward, out of its grip. After a hesitation, they shot forward with a jerk, heading fast toward the downed tree, whose tip was submerged completely. Alison slid her paddle along the hull of the canoe, braced her hands on the gunwales, and launched herself out of the boat with a belly flop. Her motion rocked the canoe so hard it half-tipped, then righted itself with more water in it. The current pushed her immediately into the tree. She protected her face with her arms and managed to grab some branches. When she looked toward shore, she saw a person face down in the water, entangled in branches and partially beneath the tree trunk.

Alison inched her way along the tree, holding onto the branches. The current tugged at her legs, trying to drag her down and under. She could feel other branches beneath the water and was afraid she'd get sucked down and trapped.

"Hey," she yelled. "Hang on."

The person didn't move. Seeing long hair floating around the helmet, she guessed it was a woman. Alison pulled herself onto the slippery trunk of the cedar and crawled along it. She reached the woman and with one hand tried to yank her free by the collar of her life vest. It didn't work. She climbed past her and tried from the other side. They were only fifteen feet from the bank. She decided the only way to get enough force was to stand on the bottom, if it was shallow enough, brace herself against the tree for leverage, and pull the woman toward her—without slipping or getting her feet snared.

The rocks were slick under the water, but the current was weaker near the shore and the water was only a few feet deep. She got her right arm under the woman's chest, clenched the vest collar with her left hand, and managed to pull her a few inches sideways and back against the push of the water. She tried again and slipped. As she went underwater, she felt herself sliding beneath the tree. She let go of the collar and grabbed a branch. She held on, then worked her feet back under herself, and came up coughing water. She stood and tried again, but this time she also pushed the body downward until she felt the resistance of the vest's flotation. The woman popped up and into Alison's arms.

"Give her to me."

Lafleur had got the canoe to shore about thirty yards downstream and run up to help. He worked his way out along the tree and took the woman from Alison. She was small, maybe a hundred pounds wet. He laid her on the bank on her back and began compressions on her abdomen. On the third push, she emitted a gush of water. But she didn't cough; she lay limp. Alison felt the woman's neck for a carotid pulse.

"I think she has a pulse. I'll do the breaths. Can you do the compressions?"

They did CPR for almost fifteen minutes, taking turns pushing on the woman's breastbone and trying to blow air into her lungs. When two rafting guides arrived, they took over. It seemed clear, after a half-hour, that the woman was dead and the would-be rescuers were getting ragged from their efforts. Then the guide from her raft showed up, along with her fellow passengers. Two others in that boat had fallen into the river at the Bus Stop. The guide, only a kid, had fished the other two out below and had expected her to turn up as well. A guide in another raft had seen her stuck in the tree and paddled upstream to throw the rope at her. A third guide caught up with the kid a hundred yards downstream and told him his client was caught in a strainer. It took the kid and his other passengers ten minutes to get organized and paddle back.

He looked like he was going to cry. The others in the group, all men, looked shocked. They weren't any happier when some of the other river guides told them they'd have to take the woman with them down to North River in the raft, that there was no point waiting for the rangers to come now.

"I don't think so," Wallace said. "I think you other guys should head down there and make a phone call. They're going to want to see where this happened and talk to people. Under the circumstances they might bring a helicopter in and paramedics. We'll stay. You, kiddo, you and your raft should stay. They're going to want to talk to you."

"You know, Wallace, the river's dropping again," another longtime guide pointed out. "We'll all need that water to get down to North River. Even you and your canoe. I don't think there's any mystery here. She fell out and got stuck in a strainer. And she drowned. I don't think anybody should wait."

The guides carried the woman about fifty yards through the woods and down to the raft she'd come in, which was tied up there. They laid her between the big inflated thwarts near the back, just ahead of the guide, covering her with jackets. The other four rafters sat farther up and seemed to have trouble focusing on the task before them. The guide, an eighteen-year-old the others knew only as Randy, called out paddling instructions to little effect. By the time they reached the takeout, two rangers were there, along with an ambulance, a fire truck, and a dozen volunteer firefighters. And then a state trooper arrived, with his emergency lights flashing.

The firefighters put the woman on a stretcher and wheeled her to the ambulance, which turned on its siren briefly as it left to warn the firefighters and rafters milling around. The rangers asked questions. They and the trooper started writing down information for reports. When the interviews were over, the others who had been in the dead woman's boat jumped in a minivan and headed back to New York City. Wallace and Alison helped Randy load his paddles, helmets, and boat on a trailer. Then Donny came in the pickup. On the drive to Newcomb, Wallace told him what had happened.

Alison was too tired to return to her aunt's cabin that evening and asked to stay at the B&B.

"No guests tonight," Wallace said. "You can have any room you want."

"I think I want to stay with you," she said.

"I'd like that."

Donny went home after one drink, and Wallace unpacked the gear while Alison took a shower. She stayed in a long time, shampooing her hair twice. Afterward, she pulled on sweatpants and a T-shirt that he left for her. Wallace later found her curled up under the quilt in his bed. He watched her sleep. She didn't move at all. He rested a hand lightly on her shoulder, then curled around her and held her in his arms, sleeping that way until morning.

22

The jangling of the phone woke Lafleur at 6:45 a.m. The caller laid into him with no preamble.

"Where the hell's my niece?"

"Lottie?"

"You better not have hurt her. Where the hell is she?"

"She's right here," Wallace said softly, running a hand through his hair. "She's sleeping."

"Put her on the goddamn phone. She was supposed to come home last night and she didn't. So I came up here this morning and people are telling me that a woman drowned in the river yesterday. So what the hell am I supposed to think?"

"I apologize, Lottie. We probably should have done something else and let you know. That's not easy considering where you live. It was a long, bad day, and Alison was too tired to get home. But she's okay. In fact, she's the one who pulled the woman out of the water. I never saw anything like it."

"And you never will again. Next time you come by my cabin with a stupid idea, you won't be welcome. I don't have time for this nonsense. Now put her on the phone."

He climbed the loft carrying the old rotary phone, which had a long cord, set the it on the quilt, and held out the receiver while gently nudging Alison, who was asleep on her stomach, her head turned away.

"You have a phone call. Alison."

"Who is it?"

He held the receiver to her face, and she said hello.

"Damn it, girl, I've been worried all night," Lottie said, loud enough for Wallace to hear.

"I'm okay," Alison said. "I tried to save someone, but she died. It wasn't good. I'm sorry, Aunt Lottie. I didn't mean to worry you."

"As long as you're okay," she said, more softly.

"I am. I'm just tired."

"Come home."

"I will. Later. Thanks for calling. I'm sorry I worried you."

Lafleur took the phone and climbed back down.

"Lottie, I'm going to let her sleep. Brave girl. She jumped in the river and got the woman untangled from a tree in the water and got her to shore. She nearly saved her. Anyway, I'm going to let her sleep the day if she wants. I've got a trip, but I'm going to bring her to you this evening. So don't worry."

"Don't give me any more cause to worry."

Lafleur kept his word. He recruited Donny to drive the van with the food, set up lunch, and collect equipment at the takeout. When they got back to his B&B about 5 p.m., Alison had caught up on her sleep. She and Wallace drove to Newcomb in the pickup, borrowed a motorboat, and got to the cabin well before dusk. Lottie made coffee and demanded to hear the whole story. They took turns in the telling.

"I don't want you canoeing there anymore," Lottie finally said.

"That wasn't the problem," Alison said. "We actually got the hang of it after a while. But I probably won't go again, at least not this season."

She winked at her aunt and smiled at Lafleur. "What else can we do for you, Aunt Lottie?"

"Besides staying out of trouble? Nothing. I have to finish this report about those spruce grouse. It was due at the agency last week, and I'm late. But I didn't get any sleep last night for worrying. And I didn't get any work done today."

"Tell you what," Alison said. "I'm going to stay at the B&B for a few days and get out of your hair so you can get your work done. I promise I won't go back out on the river all week, except maybe in a raft. Come get me when you're done."

Lafleur said nothing.

"Is that okay with you?" Alison asked him. "I'll do my laundry there and straighten that place up. It could use it."

"That's fine."

She packed her clothes and took her bow and arrows. When they reached the B&B, she hung her bow in the equipment room and carried her duffel bag into Lafleur's room.

23

The first thing Jack Kirkland did was drive to the rafting company and ask for a copy of the waiver the dead woman had signed. Artie, Kirkland's boss at Acme Insured, had said to forget everything else, that this was the single most important piece of business. So Kirkland got up at dawn, reviewed the file, and arrived at the rafting company's headquarters, a converted house a little beyond North Creek, by 9 a.m. The door was propped open, and a sign out front boasted, "Whitewater Big Time/More Fun Than You Can Handle." The sign no doubt would interest the lawyer for Wilson Art & Design who had contacted Artie on Monday. They were filing a negligence claim.

The dead woman, Jeanie Jones, had been on a company outing. Artie said the design outfit was, first, covering its ass for organizing an outing where somebody could get killed. Second, well, look at the sign, Kirkland thought. It screamed: Sue me! The actual insurance policy, which Artie had sold and maintained, belonged to a carrier out of Des Moines. Their research staff had looked into New York State's liability laws concerning waivers. The first question, the most important one, was whether she had signed one acknowledging she understood the risky nature of the outing and promised to hold the company harmless. The second, which would take some sorting out, was whether the rafting company had done something wrong. The owner, John Morgan, assured Kirkland over the phone that it had not. The woman was wearing a flotation vest, which was properly buckled, and a helmet. She'd received the same safety briefing that the guides give all rafters.

Morgan wasn't in immediate jeopardy of losing his policy, but if he did, it could put him out of business. There were only three companies writing such policies in the Adirondacks, and Artie Marder sold all of them at his insurance agency. But Artie told Kirkland to spend some time on the case, give Morgan's operation a close look and see if his methods were "unsound"— a pet expression he'd picked up from *Apocalypse Now*, the movie about a patrol boat's journey upriver into the jungle during the Vietnam War. Kirkland hadn't seen it but remembered liking Conrad's *Heart of Darkness*, the novel the movie was loosely based on. Having spent three years in the army, he didn't watch movies about the military, even when they came on TV. Not interested. But the movie and the book raised an interesting question: Could you, like Conrad's Kurtz, go native in a place like this, just ninety miles from so-called civilization, and never go back?

Parked behind the house were a half-dozen old school buses with green-and-blue inflatable rafts strapped to the roofs. Other rafts were stacked on a rack nearby. Kirkland returned to the front of the building and entered the front door, where a kid stood behind the counter. His hair was tied in a ponytail. He smiled and asked if he could help. Morgan had left copies of all five waivers signed by the rafting group from Wilson Art & Design, including Jeanie Jones's. They looked all right, with names filled out, appropriate spots initialed, and signatures at the end. Kirkland asked to see the originals, which the kid produced from Morgan's files in the back, and they matched. Artie had made a point of telling him to do that, see the originals, so there wouldn't be any bad surprises. The kid faxed the waivers to Artie and let Kirkland use the phone to make sure they got there. The old man reminded Kirkland to look around and ask questions, including the obvious ones. Kirkland had come early, knowing Morgan didn't usually show up until later.

"Who was the guide in the raft?" he asked the counter kid, a slender teenager named Dylan who smiled a lot. He was a good choice for the counter, the first disarmingly genial contact for customers who might not be sure they wanted to brave a little adventure on the river.

"It was Randy."

"Is he around?"

"Yeah, he's in the campground. His is the blue tent."

Morgan let his guides camp for free in an open area behind a pole barn. On this morning, there were a half-dozen tents set up around a fire pit, with gear, muddy boots, and wet sneakers piled outside. The blue tent was a small dome, with a mesh window on one side and a zippered-shut door on the other. Kirkland bent down by the window and saw a rumpled sleeping bag inside. He said Randy's name a few times before getting a response.

"Yeah. I'm coming." The zipper opened, and the boy climbed out. He had close-cropped dark hair and a hint of a mustache. He wore wrinkled jeans and a green T-shirt with the rafting company's logo on it.

"Randy?"

"Yeah. What's up?"

"I'm from the insurance company. I need to talk to you for a minute."

"All right."

"Why don't we sit down? It won't take long." Kirkland walked over to a log bench beside the fire pit and seated himself. The teenager sat down next to him. He was average height, almost as slender as the counter kid, but quieter, more reserved.

"First, I need to check. You were guiding last week when the woman fell out and drowned."

"I was. I mean, yeah. I didn't mean for that to happen. It was an accident." He looked up. "By the time I knew what happened, she was way upriver, in a strainer. I don't know how she got there. It wasn't even close to where we were."

Kirkland handed him the waivers, and he confirmed that he'd explained them and that the clients each signed one. Morgan himself had done the safety briefing right there on the grassy lot, next to the buses, the way they always did it. The woman had been really excited and said she'd been rafting before. She seemed in charge of the group.

"She kept telling me she really wanted to rock. She wasn't scared at all. She said she'd been swimming before, and she kept teasing the other guys that they were going to find out what that was like."

"So you rocked."

"Well, yeah. It's kind of the thing here. If people don't swim it's not a good trip. But nobody ever got hurt before. I mean, sometimes scrapes and bruises, but that's it. And everybody's still smiling. How do you drown with a life vest? And I made sure they were all on tight. And a helmet, so I don't see how she could've got knocked out or anything. It's not actually that dangerous. Except maybe if you're old."

"How old do you think she was?" Artie's notes from his phone call with the lawyer indicated she was fifty-seven.

"I don't know. Old. Not ancient."

"But not too old for rafting?"

"She could paddle. And she was bouncing all over the place before we got going. She couldn't sit still. Kind of like a little kid. And once we got going, we'd hit a wave or something pretty hard and she kept saying, 'Is that all you've got?' Like she wanted me to ramp it up."

"So you did."

"Yeah, but not that much. No more than usual, really."

"What did you make of that, all the enthusiasm?"

"I think she was kind of trying to pump up the guys she was with," he said. "It was kind of a nerdy bunch. They weren't saying much. I don't know."

Randy explained that the place where Jeanie Jones fell out, the Bus Stop, was the last big feature in the run, a hydraulic behind a rock where the water sucked way down and stayed there for a while before coming back up. They went almost straight over it. The woman and two of the guys in the raft fell out. He'd told them to hold on. The boat was stuck there for only a few seconds, he said, then the bow popped up and they continued downstream. The two customers still in the raft helped him stop and turn in the flat water below, where they picked up the other two swimmers. They waited ten minutes for Jennie Jones to show up before a guide from another company asked if they were missing somebody and said there was somebody stuck in a tree. They paddled upstream, took out below the strainer, and walked up to where people had gathered.

"They were doing CPR and then they quit doing it 'cause it wasn't doing any good. She didn't look dead. It didn't seem possible."

24

At the state offices in Ray Brook, Kirkland collected copies of the incident reports written by the rangers and the trooper. None of the reports' writers were around, but another ranger told him where he could find W. Lafleur, identified as the person who found Jeanie Jones. He drove back through Lake Placid, got slowed again in the peak-season crawl of traffic on Main Street, and then wound along the two-lane highway until he saw the wooden sign for Lafleur Whitewater Expeditions and B&B and turned onto a dirt driveway that looped through the trees.

Alison was loading the van, dragging a plastic cooler through the dust toward the open side door. She looked up briefly, smiled, then walked across a patch of grass and into the door of the bed-and-breakfast. She came out a minute later hoisting a second cooler down the step and plopped it on the ground.

"Give me a hand, would you?" she said.

"Sure." Kirkland walked quickly across the driveway.

"Grab that handle. I need to put it in the van."

It was surprisingly heavy to him. It seemed unlikely she'd lifted it by herself.

"What's in this, rocks?"

"Rocks. Funny. It's food. Some people like to eat a lot, and we aim to keep the customers satisfied." They lifted the cooler into the van, and she slid it to one side. "Now I could use a hand with the other one."

They hoisted the other cooler up, next to the first one. It was even heavier.

"Beverages."

"How were you going to get this in by yourself?" Kirkland asked.

"A complex series of pulleys and levers, which I keep in my pocket for just such occasions."

"Don't think there's any room there." He'd noticed the tight denim cutoffs, long brown legs, and dusty flip-flops.

She was pulling the van's sliding door closed and stopped and looked at him, smiling slightly. "And how would you know that?"

He figured she was somewhere in her twenties, about his age, and not wearing any rings. Her long light-brown hair was pulled back in a loose pony-tail that spread and curled down her shoulders. The oxfordcloth shirt, pale blue, had its sleeves neatly rolled up, with the tails tied together above her abdomen.

He was taken by surprise by the challenging, maybe joking, remark, but wasn't embarrassed. "To tell you the truth, it doesn't look like you're hiding much."

"And do you have a problem with that?"

"No. Not at all."

"Good. Because it's going to be hot today. And I'm not dressing to please you. No offense intended. Who are you, by the way?"

"Jack Kirkland, Acme Insured."

"Oh really. Are you trying to sell me some kind of insurance policy, Jack Kirkland, Acme Insured?"

"No. Nothing like that."

"That's good. Because your pitch isn't working."

"I'm sorry. I didn't mean to say anything to offend you. The truth is you look great, and I shouldn't have said anything."

"Now there's an equivocally chauvinist response, Jack Kirkland, Acme Insured. Is that a made-up name? It sounds like one. What do you want?"

"The fact is you mentioned your pocket first."

"Typical man," Alison said. "Blame it on the woman every time. You just keep moving backwards, don't you?"

"Is W. Lafleur here?"

"That's not precisely a name familiar to me. But if it were why are you asking?"

Kirkland couldn't tell whether she was irritated, playing with him, or telling the truth, all the time looking him right in the eye. He explained why he'd come, that Lafleur's name was on the rangers' report as the one who'd found a woman dead on the upper Hudson River, and that he simply wanted to talk to him.

"You might be looking for Wallace Lafleur. Is that it?"

"Was he on the Hudson River in the town of Minerva on July 11th?"

"I believe so."

"Is he here?"

"He's probably on the Hudson River in the town of Minerva right about now. You have a lot of questions, Jack Kirkland, Acme Insured. And I've got to go. I'm going to be late."

She walked to the door of the building, locked it, walked back, and opened the door to the driver's side of the van, with Kirkland standing next to it.

"He'll be back later. By five, anyway," Alison said. "Or you can call him. The business number is listed."

25

The young rafters had explained how the whitewater trips worked, usually with lunch at the end at one of the roadside turnouts in North River, where the serious rapids ended and the Hudson emerged from the wilderness and ran alongside the road. Kirkland was pretty sure the woman was headed there, and it was on his way home anyway. He had the option of staying and nosing around for a day or two and decided there was nothing to be lost from lazing away the afternoon in the sunshine, since it was dry, breezy, quiet, with the air sweetly and faintly scented by the trees. He pulled a tall, slender stem of grass and slid it in his mouth, threw his sportcoat and tie into the back of the subcompact, then produced a pen and wrote down the license number of the van.

He got in and drove down Route 73 to old Route 9 and followed it south and then followed signs for turnoffs to North Creek and North River. He hadn't known which exit to take off the four-lane highway and thought this way there'd be a chance to look around, not get lost, and still get there long before the woman and Lafleur had finished up and gone. Based on what he'd been told, they'd have to feed their rafters, get them changed and dry, and return them to wherever they left their cars. He was pretty sure the woman he met was bringing the lunch and trying to get rid of him. He vaguely hoped to see her again. Some of her remarks were just banter. But there was a sharp edge there. It was defensive, not altogether friendly.

When he found them, lunch was winding down. The two families, including four children, had eaten at the picnic tables and changed clothes in a tent set up for the purpose. They had left both of their minivans up the road and were now about ready to go. The crimson inflatable raft was loaded on its trailer behind a black pickup. Kirkland saw a man with shaggy black hair and heavy stubble sitting in the cab, with a clipboard out. He had the door open and was talking to a woman holding four brightly colored T-shirts with river logos.

"So we'll just add these in and keep it on your credit card," the man said.

"Okay. I think that's all we've got."

"Well, you know, if you change your mind later we've got more."

"Thank you. That was great. We had a great time." She reached in and gave him a hug.

"We aim to please," he said. "Now I'm going to go back to the put-in, and I need the drivers of both of your vehicles so they can come back down here and get everybody else. So please you get them and make sure they've got their keys, and then we can go."

The woman walked toward her group, calling for her husband. Kirkland approached the pickup.

"Wallace Lafleur?"

"Yes, I am."

"Jack Kirkland. I'm hoping to talk to you about the accident last week." He stuck out a hand, and Lafleur shook it.

"Alison told me you'd come around. I'd be happy to talk to you, but I'm a little busy at the moment. See, I've got to get these people back up to their cars so they can come back and get their families. So I don't really have time now."

Alison walked up behind Kirkland. "You followed me," she said.

"Not really. I just followed Route 9 and then the signs to North Creek. Some other rafters told me where the rafts come off the river."

"It's called the takeout," she said. She told Lafleur, "He says I look great."

"Hard to argue with that. You do look great," Wallace said. "It brightens my day. But here's the thing. I do have to go. I'll be happy to talk to you later. What you could do is help Alison clean up, and you can talk to her. She was actually there. She is not only beautiful, she's heroic. And later, if you still have questions, you can talk to me. You can come by. You can call me. Whatever you want."

The two husbands traipsed up, one still eating a sandwich, the other drinking a soda, and Lafleur made sure they had their keys. They got in the passenger side of the pickup, and Lafleur eased the vehicle out of the turnout and headed north on Route 28, pulling the trailer and colorful raft behind.

The wives sat at the picnic table, one smoking, while the children rummaged among the cake and cookies for second desserts or wandered down the grassy bank to throw stones or look for small fish in the shallows of the river. Kirkland helped Alison clear the table, throwing paper plates into a trash bag, collecting soda cans for another bag, and packing up the bread, chips, condiments, cold cuts, and cheeses. She stored all the food and neatly packed the coolers, which were lighter now, and he helped her put them in the van. While they took down the tent, he finally asked her if she was there, and she said yes.

"It's not a great subject," she said. "It was pretty unpleasant. I'm not spending a lot of time thinking about it. On purpose. But first tell me what you want to know and why. I mean, what's your point? Why do you need to know? What are you trying to prove?"

"I'm not actually trying to prove anything. I'm just trying to find out what happened. There's an insurance claim, and I'm just trying to find out how it fits with what actually did happen."

"Can I get in trouble for trying to help her?"

"No. Not when you're just a passer-by. As a Good Samaritan you can't. That's the way the law works. Even if by trying to help her you did something that inadvertently contributed to her dying. You can't get in trouble for that."

"All right. That's what Wallace said, too. I'll tell you what I know. But first, who's the claim against?"

"The company whose raft she fell out of."

"Right. I didn't see how she fell in. When we saw her she was all by herself, stuck in a tree. Her face was in the water. It's called a strainer. They should probably file the claim against the tree."

26

Wilson Art & Design agreed to give Kirkland a single meeting with the four graphic artists who'd been in the raft with Jeanie Jones. The company occupied offices in a building at Park and 34th Street in Manhattan. The bustle and the elevators made him feel like he was in a cheerful movie from the fifties, perhaps starring Cary Grant. But the once-stylish office space on the seventeenth floor had long ago been partitioned into cubicles with movable, interchangeable, fabric-covered dividers, enclosing drawing tables and desktop computers. He was surprised that a company that relied on creativity would have such a gray, institutional workplace. It was cheesy and cramped.

The meeting was held in a windowless conference room at the end of the floor. The human-resources manager—Ms. Fitzhue, a brusque woman in a cream-colored suit—sat in and took notes. Initially, she had refused his request to talk to the others, but Kirkland made it clear that no claim could be resolved until then. She next insisted that she and the company's counsel be allowed to attend. Artie said all of that was fine. What were they going to do, sue his Acme agency? They'd already made the claim. A lawsuit would take years and cost them thousands of dollars. He predicted no lawyer would show up, that they wouldn't spend the money and would instead set up the meeting quickly, and he proved right on both counts.

After Fitzhue ushered Kirkland into the room, she returned five minutes later with the artists, all men, three probably in their twenties or early thirties, the fourth about a decade older and balding. He had their names from the waivers they'd signed and took a minute to confirm which was which and began taking notes on a legal pad. The older one, Maloney, gave him a hard look. The skinny blond-haired guy in a T-shirt, Van Peltz, brought a small notebook, which he opened to a blank page, and began sketching. The last two slumped and looked at the table. White was tall with a large head. Reynolds was shorter, with a small mustache. All looked like they couldn't wait to leave. The second thing Kirkland did was pass each one his waiver and ask if he had signed it, which they all acknowledged.

"Did Jeanie Jones sign one too?"

Nobody answered. Maloney shrugged.

"You all got the safety talk, right?"

"That's the part about don't stand up if you fall in the water?" Reynolds asked. "Which if you ask me is a crazy idea. What if you fall out where it's really shallow? I asked that question. They didn't have an answer."

"What I'm trying to get at is you all got the safety talk and Jeanie Jones did, too. And you all wore life vests, which were properly buckled. And she did, too. That's what the guide said, and unless you tell me otherwise, I believe him. And you all wore helmets."

"You have one of those forms with her name on it, right?" Van Peltz asked, looking up from his doodling, the pencil still poised over what looked like an exotic frog. "You know she signed it. Why ask us?"

"I just need to be sure, that's all," Kirkland said. "That's the first thing. The second is I need to know what happened."

"She fell out. Then the next thing is we're paddling back upstream to get her," Reynolds said. "That's all I know."

"So you were in the raft the whole time?"

"What do you mean?"

"Did you fall out of the raft?" Kirkland asked him directly. He was pretty sure they were being deliberately unhelpful, and it was probably because of the HR woman. They didn't want to get in trouble with the company.

"Yes, I fell out of the raft. Jim did too." Van Peltz didn't look up from his sketch pad when his name was mentioned.

"Then what happened?"

"We went under, then we floated back up, and we started floating downstream, and the raft picked us up," Reynolds said.

"Did you lose your paddles?"

"I kept mine. That's what you're supposed to do," Reynolds said. He pointed to Van Peltz. "He didn't."

Kirkland let the silence continue for a minute and jotted notes. He looked at Van Peltz and asked what had happened to him. He stopped sketching and laid down the pencil.

"We were coming into this place that the guide said was the biggest thing on the river. The raft went nose down, and I fell out. The next thing I know I'm underwater. I looked up, and it felt like the water was sucking me down, and I could see the bottom of the raft. It was right over me. Right on top of me. And then the raft moved 'cause I could see sunlight. And then I came up, like I was shot out of a gun. That's what happened to me. And then I saw Lee, who was just in front of me."

"Where were you sitting in the raft?"

"Right in front. I tried to hold onto the rope, but it didn't do any good. It happened too fast."

"Where were you sitting?" he asked Reynolds.

"I don't know. Second row, I guess. We switched several times where we were sitting."

"Where was Jeanie Jones?"

"I don't know."

"Does anybody know?"

"She was next to me," Van Peltz said. "She was in front."

Kirkland kept writing.

"Where were you guys?" he asked Maloney and White.

"In the third seat," Maloney said.

"So you were able to hold on?"

"Obviously."

"Did the guide, Randy, did he warn you?"

"He said, 'Hang on,'" Maloney replied. "The raft went nose down, like Jim said. Then after a while it popped back up. After that we kept going downstream, and we stopped. And these guys showed up a few minutes later, and we pulled them in."

"Did the guide seem to know what he was doing?"

"He was young," Maloney said. "He didn't panic or anything like that. He seemed to know something about it."

"Do you think he tipped the raft on purpose?"

"Jeanie kept telling him to," Reynolds said. "She kept saying, 'Hit it harder.' So I think he did what he was told."

"Was it reckless?"

"I don't know," Reynolds said. "All I know is that I got thrown out."

"Did you think you could have drowned?"

"I could have easily been killed without the life vest," Van Peltz said.

"So what do you think happened to Jeanie Jones?"

"They said she got stuck in a tree," Van Peltz said. "I didn't see it."

"You didn't see her at all?"

He stopped doing cross-hatching on the exotic frog's back.

"I didn't see her at all after I fell out."

"What about you guys?"

Maloney and Smith said they didn't see her after the raft righted itself. Reynolds looked down, shaking his head. It looked less to Kirkland like he was saying no than responding to some other question, an internal dialogue with himself.

"You don't recall seeing her?" Kirkland asked him.

"I don't recall what I saw. It happened pretty fast, and then I was underwater and it was hard to see anything."

27

While starting to gather his things, Kirkland asked the artists about the woman who died, though Artie had warned him not to get too personal, to keep that part abstract and unemotional. Stay professional, he said. Don't stir the pot.

"What was she like?"

"We didn't know her that well," Reynolds said. "She was here, what, less than two years. I don't think any of us socialized with her except at these company functions."

"You did this kind of thing a lot?"

"No. Not a lot. Jim, how many times do you think we did something like this?"

"Three times," Van Peltz said. "Bowling, hiking, and this one."

"Oh, that's right. I forgot about the bowling," Reynolds said. "That was ... interesting. I don't know where she came up with this stuff."

"Rafting was her idea too?"

"Completely. She'd been rafting before. She even made us watch the video. And the crazy thing was, she fell out of that raft. This was somewhere in Colorado. And she's all excited about it. Then she makes us watch it. The video. And then she makes us do it. It was crazy."

Ms. Fitzhue interrupted. "I think that's irrelevant," she said, giving Reynolds a sharp look. Kirkland made notes and asked if they had a copy of the videotape. Fitzhue said they didn't; it was Jeanie Jones's personal property.

He asked Maloney what he thought about the outings, and he replied that he was the wrong person to ask. With some prodding it came out that he'd been the boss of that little unit until Jeanie Jones arrived, and he didn't think much of her methods.

"Would you say her methods were unsound?"

"Obviously," Maloney replied. "Look at what happened."

White appeared lost in thought but when pressed said he believed getting out of the office was a good idea once in a while.

"I liked bowling," he said.

"What about rafting?"

"That was fun. Until the end."

Fitzhue said they had work to do and if Kirkland had further questions, he could contact her.

"Let me ask you guys one last question. Did you like her?"

This time Maloney shook his head, frowning. White looked off into space. Van Peltz focused on his sketch with new concentration.

"Let me tell you one story," Reynolds said. "Every Saturday one of us has to come in and get some proofs together that have to be packaged up and sent out to the printer for our big client. They set up their press on the weekend, and the run begins first thing Monday morning. So we've got a copier over there that I'm using to fix some things that have to get overnight delivered, and I'm back at my desk for a minute and she comes in and sets all my stuff over to one side, in a pile. And I come back, and she's copying something of hers, some side project. She's not even supposed to be here on Saturday. And she's doing her own stuff. And I say, 'What's going on here?' And she says, 'Oh, am I in your way? I'll only be a minute.' And it took her an hour, and the overnight stuff was almost late to the printer. I'm sorry, Margaret, but she was freelancing out of here all the time. You guys thought you brought in this prize-winning design genius to reinvent us. And that's what you got. Jeanie Jones was all about Jeanie Jones. And that's a fact. Does anybody here disagree with me?"

None of the other artists looked up. Fitzhue seemed at a loss for words as well.

"Thank you," Kirkland said. "I'll be in touch."

28

Alison hadn't liked Kirkland despite herself. She admitted later that he reminded her, almost right away, of Will. Both were about six feet tall with broad shoulders, square-jawed, as if stepping out of her girlhood version of Central Casting for guy. Her first reaction was the old one, to smile. Her second was what she felt when she left New York, which was wariness and even a recollection of fear. The third, which was the one that was sticking around, was genial hostility. There's a combination, she thought. The very essence of sarcasm. She came to realize that he posed no threat. Kirkland hadn't come to get her or Wallace in trouble. And he was nice enough, respectful even, whether or not that was just a professional veneer. So why had she mocked him? It took her two days of thinking about it on and off to put the correct psychological term to it: reaction formation.

The truth was she found him kind of attractive, and she could see from the way he looked at her that he thought she was. He'd even tried to flirt, in a typically male ham-handed way. He wasn't a subtle guy. He was young. Dull normal, in the parlance. Unlike Wallace, whom she trusted and yet still couldn't entirely read. Who radiated goodwill and joy. She had crawled inside that bubble of love and basked in it, absorbed it, embraced it, and even started to radiate it back to the world. It had happened gradually over weeks. Trying to save the woman in the river felt mainly like an extension of it. She felt safe with Wallace, yet life with him was also adventurous, physically thrilling, satisfying that way, and she was pretty sure that she was starting to love this man. And it was totally unacceptable to find this other guy attractive at all. It was probably just a function of being open to the world and all its wonders, the thing Wallace preached, and totally contrary to everything her mother ever drilled into her. And what would her mother think of Wallace Lafleur? There was an unpleasant question. Probably the same thing she thought about Lottie. Another heathen who'd gone native. Her mother's words. The last thing Alison wanted in her head. She felt great. And she looked good. You could see it in Wallace's eyes and in the looks from Kirkland and other men. Wallace exhibited no jealousy whatsoever. But Alison didn't like the feeling about Kirkland and turned it into something more acceptable, irritation, and expressed it.

When Kirkland phoned the morning after he visited Manhattan, saying he had a few other things he wanted to ask her and Wallace about, she put him off immediately.

"You haven't actually talked to Wallace yet, right?"

"That's right."

"Then call him later. He'll be back after five." Alison prepared to hang up.

"This being Friday, he's probably got another rafting trip tomorrow. And he's going to be busy when he gets back."

"Probably."

"So he probably wouldn't call me tonight, and he'll call back sometime on his free day, which I'm guessing might be sometime next week, right?" Kirkland said.

"That's genius."

"So if I'm going to talk to him before then, whenever that is, I'll probably have to come back up there."

Alison now felt completely annoyed. "I don't think that's necessary. He'll call you when he can."

But Kirkland said he was looking at a weekend with no plans. He figured if nothing else he'd talk to Lafleur and bring his old sleeping bag and maybe hike somewhere in the mountains and sleep under the stars. When he told Alison that he'd probably see her later, she hung up.

29

No one answered his knock at the B&B, so Kirkland began walking the property. The loaded trailer, pickup truck, and van were all there. When he heard the soft sound of voices, he followed it through the trees to a clearing. Alison and Wallace were sitting in wooden armchairs next to a small circle of stones with a stack of kindling inside it. They looked up briefly, and Wallace nodded.

"We're just having a glass of wine," he said. "Pull up a chair."

Kirkland sat in the hand-hewn chair next to Alison and said hello. She lifted up her stemmed glass and sipped. "I thought you were going to call," she said.

"Well, you're here now," Wallace said. "Do you want some wine?"

"Sure. Thank you."

Lafleur said he'd be right back, that he'd get another glass. Then Alison said she'd go instead.

"Thank you, darlin'."

"You're welcome." Alison stood up, stretched slowly, then walked behind Lafleur's chair, rested her hands on his shoulders, and kissed the dark curls on the top of his head. "Anything else?"

"I don't think so at the moment. But I do appreciate that."

She walked toward the house, and they watched her go.

"Life is good," Lafleur said, and he laughed.

Dusk was beginning to settle, the sun muffled at the edge of an overcast sky. Kirkland slapped his neck where an insect bit him. "I thought blackfly season was supposed to be over."

"It is. What bit you was a mosquito. Same as you have down in Albany."

"How do you know?"

"Well, as a woodsman I can tell the difference. I can see a mosquito." Lafleur smiled. "This will help."

He pulled a wooden match out of his pocket, stood, struck the match on the arm of his chair, cupped the flame in one hand, and stooped to light the pine needles and twigs underneath the kindling. He straightened and looked at his visitor.

"There's a woodpile beside the barn. Help me get a few logs."

They walked through the trees to a five-foot-high stack of split wood topped by cut boughs of balsams, which provided a sweetly scented canopy. Wallace walked to one end of the twenty-foot stack.

"Here, these are a little drier. Put your arms out." He began stacking wood in Kirkland's arms, two pieces at a time. "Tell me when we hit your limit."

At twelve pieces, his arms grew unsteady and shook.

"I think that'll do it," Lafleur said. They returned to the campfire, where Kirkland tilted forward and let the wood clatter to the ground. He noticed that Lafleur was carrying only three pieces.

"I think we're set for a little while. Thank you," Wallace said. He laid two split logs on his kindling stack, which didn't collapse. They both sat down and watched the flames rise around the logs. "If you pull your chair a little closer, the mosquitoes won't bother you as much."

"They don't bother you?"

"No. Mainly they don't."

"What do you ascribe that to?"

"You know, Jack, I'd have to say it's something in the blood. They just don't seem to want mine. I will tell you a secret, though. Long hair and a beard. Did you ever wonder why those old mountain men had hair down to their shoulders and beards down to their chest?"

"They didn't have a razor?"

"That may be. But it kept them warm in the winter and critter-free in the summer."

"Except for the ones that nested there."

"Well, there you go. Which is why we're grateful for the modern invention of shampoo."

Alison came back dressed in warmer clothes: jeans and hiking boots, loosely tied, and a long-sleeve red flannel shirt that was too big, her hair cascading over the upturned collar. Kirkland tried not to stare.

She poured wine from the bottle by her chair into a long-stemmed wine glass and handed it to him. Then she refilled Wallace's glass and hers.

"Jack, why don't you tell me exactly what it is you're doing. How can I help you?" Lafleur said.

Kirkland explained the insurance company's position with the claim against the rafter, that they weren't sure whether the woman's company was simply trying to protect itself or seriously thought it could get some money. No family had come forward to make a life-insurance claim on behalf of Jeanie Jones, as far as they knew. He had asked their personnel director about next of kin, and she hadn't replied.

"Maybe they're just not telling you," Alison said.

"I think they'd have to. The coroner's report didn't list anybody, either. I don't think there is anybody. I think what she had was her career."

"That's sad."

"Though apparently she was quite the wild woman on the river. She kept telling the guide to hit the waves harder. And apparently he did. That's what her co-workers said, too. She'd done it before and had fallen out of a raft before, out in Colorado. Apparently it's on a video she made them watch. And she was in her late fifties. Kind of out there."

"So you can close the book on this one?" Wallace said.

"Not yet. The problem is the guide told me that they try to make it exciting. Something like 'If nobody's swimming you're not really trying' philosophy at that rafting outfit. And their advertisement even says, 'More than you can handle,' something like that. So the question is whether he was reckless."

Lafleur sighed. "I know Randy. He's local, a nice kid. I've seen him on the river. He knows how to handle a raft, get it downriver without tipping it over. Without hurting anybody. And he's done it a dozen times. So if a client keeps saying, 'Do it more, do it harder,' whose idea was it?"

"Except you wouldn't do that," Alison said.

"I wouldn't. But I've been at this a long time. There are ways you can handle a client like that."

"How?" Kirkland asked.

"You can guide the raft so you know where it will hit the wave and who's going to get wet, with the water pouring right over them. It's easiest to put that person right up front, and hit every wave right there. They don't really have to leave the raft. Pretty soon they're tired of it. You might say it dampens their enthusiasm just a little. Then you go back to what you were doing. Everybody has a great day."

"It probably takes a while to get that good."

"It does. Look, I have no idea what was going on in that raft. If they followed all the usual safety precautions—I know that operation and I'm pretty sure they did, though I don't actually know—if you're trying to prove recklessness, I don't know that you can."

"So the bottom line is your company doesn't want to pay anything. And if there's no recklessness, you do or you don't?" Alison said. "I'm not seeing it."

"I don't know, either," Kirkland said. "Truthfully. I'm new at this. She signed a waiver. Maybe that's the whole thing."

"I'm still not seeing it," Alison said, sounding impatient. "You insure the rafting company. So if they did nothing wrong, you don't pay anybody, correct? But if they were reckless, if they messed this up, then they're liable. And as their insurance company, you'd have to pay for that. Correct?"

"More or less."

"So why didn't you say so? Why are you trying to prove they messed up?"

"I'm not. But I need to find out what's true. Figure out first if there's a reasonable basis for the liability claim, so we'll know what to do. What we have to do. It could end up in court. Coming here tonight, that's extra. I didn't have anything going on this weekend. I just had to talk to you some-time. It's beautiful up here. It was an excuse to come back."

In the darkening evening, Wallace put two more logs on the fire, which cast both heat and a soft, flickering glow. Kirkland pulled his chair closer. "I like this. How did you come to be here?"

"Well, Jack, that's a long story. When I was a kid, this was in Utica, the woods were at the end of our street. I went there every chance I got. I'd come home when I was supposed to, more or less, but if you ever wanted to find me, that's where I was. It just worked out over time that I was able to live the thing I was passionate about."

"It's that simple?"

"No. It's taken years, mortgages, some of which I'm still paying. Every season I've got the stack of bills on one side of my desk and the stack of checks on the other. It usually works out. Though sometimes there's not a lot left over. Every fall I get a deer—well, just about—and that helps me get through the winter. I guide all year and rent out my house. When there's business. Fortunately, so far, there's been enough."

"You make it look easy."

Wallace poured more wine for all three of them. "Tonight it's easy."

They sat quietly for a while, watching the fire. Alison brought out a second bottle. Kirkland talked about surfing, something Wallace said he wanted to do sometime. Wallace talked about mountaineering, something Jack said he'd like to try, though he wasn't sure he was game for several days in the ice and snow of Mount McKinley. He didn't like being cold that much.

"That was my lion, my rite of passage," Lafleur said. He grew quiet. "I actually saw the curvature of the Earth. I was standing on top of the globe."

"I think the only time I ever felt anything like that was in the Greek Islands," Kirkland said. "I spent a week once on Santorini. I swam in the Aegean. I actually swam across to the volcano one morning. That was my lion, if there ever was one. I was afraid I was going to get plowed under by a cruise ship. The water was emerald blue, clear, unlike the Atlantic or Pacific or anyplace else that I've ever seen. I read the *Odyssey* there on a black-sand beach and could imagine what inspired Homer to write it. Where Western civilization began and runs in an unbroken line across nearly three thousand years. And they had so much right at the start."

"I like the mythology. The gods and especially the goddesses," Lafleur said, smiling at Alison. "All beautiful. All dangerous."

"Do you have a favorite?"

"Artemis. The huntress. An untamed spirit, fierce in the protection of small and gentle animals and the young. A fearsome shot with her bow."

"Yet sometimes vengeful and impulsive," Jack said. "If you consider what happened to Orion. Destined to become a dead lover and a constellation."

"That was an accident," Wallace said. "I would never put myself in the bow sight. Or swim where I could be mistaken for a target, or hit by a cruise ship. But it's interesting that you know that. "

"I like the Greeks," Kirkland said. "I think in some way those stories tell us who we are, who we've always been. With contradictions, of course."

"Seafarers and adventurers. Poets. Warriors," Lafleur said. "Makers of philosophy, ethics and democracy. Myths."

"Unlike the Romans, who inherited all these gifts but over the next thousand years conquered the known world and paved it," Jack replied, feeling the wine.

"Watch out," Wallace said. "My mother's Italian."

"So if you're so inspired, why are you here and not there?" Alison said.

"Lack of wit, imagination, and money. I had the fortune to be born in the third generation in the Americas. I'm not finished with the New World yet. What about you?"

"She's a psychologist," Wallace said. "I have no doubt that one day she'll be a doctor. Ask her a question about psychology. You'll be amazed."

"Why don't I call my mother more?" Jack said. "Please don't tell me it's Freudian."

"Forget it," Alison said. "I don't have that kind of time. Do you think you're going to uncover everything you haven't understood about your family because I tell you four things? Go find a book and educate yourself."

Lafleur laughed. "There will be no analysis for you," he said.

Stung, Kirkland challenged her. "Okay, then tell me the value of psychology. If you can."

Alison filled her glass, held it up, and watched the firelight refract in it. "Here it is. The universe is knowable. It can be known by mankind through the slow process of the scientific method if we continue to chip away at it. Cognitive dissonance explains most everything about people. And psychodynamic theory explains the rest. How's that."

"Amazing." He aimed for irony, but missed. It sounded more like admiration. "What else?"

"Art is more important than science. We should run the schools so that students know that science is there to support art, the supreme achievement of humanity. Oh, and human nature is essentially good. If you start from that assumption all manner of things will be well. Anyway, those are the things that come to mind immediately."

"What's psychodynamic theory?"

"You'll have to look it up."

"Brilliant and fierce," Wallace said. "Like an ancient Greek."

Alison shook her head and laughed. Kirkland asked them to tell him their stories, and both did, listening carefully to each other. They didn't ask for his, even when he mentioned he was also from Utica. They listened to the night sounds, an undercurrent of crickets and the crackling of the fire. Alison was having trouble putting a name to how she felt, then thought that this was what was meant by high summer and it should continue indefinitely. Lafleur called Kirkland their guest and said he could camp out next to the fire and probably shouldn't drive. Wallace was cautious about happiness that came very specifically from people, that wasn't organic, from inside, or a function of where and how he lived, always reaching for the sublime. Yet here it was. He admitted it.

They burned all the logs, got more in the dark, burned those, and sometime well after midnight Alison and Wallace went to bed. Jack unrolled his sleeping bag near the fire and crawled in.

When they got inside the bedroom, Alison reached for Lafleur immediately, buried his mouth under hers, stepped out of her boots, and unbuttoned her shirt, dropping it to the floor. She did the same for him, never breaking the kiss. She unsnapped and unzipped her jeans and slid them off, and his as well. Only then did she step back and look at him and smile at how much he wanted her.

"Wait," she said. "I want to get on the bed."

She climbed onto the loft, and he followed. They didn't go to sleep until somewhere near dawn. Lafleur wondered in passing if her desire, which felt more reckless and intense than usual, was partly informed by the wine and maybe even the attention of another man. That didn't worry him particularly. It had always been his position that people were with him when they chose to be, and otherwise they weren't. And if he never had another night exactly like this one, with the woman he was pretty sure he wanted to never leave, he'd had one. And for that, he was grateful.

30

Kirkland awoke stiff and tried to slide deeper into the sleeping bag. He thought for a moment about where he was and decided to get going, try to see something more of the mountains. He rolled up the bag, put his sneakers back on, and checked his pockets to make sure his wallet and keys hadn't fallen out and into the bag during the night. The fire was out, just ashes inside the circle of stones. The air was still, and it felt like the day was going to be warm. There were only a few high clouds, and the sun was not yet above the horizon in the southeast. His vague plan was to drive down to the trailheads for Mount Marcy and Algonquin, thinking he might try to climb one or the other. He didn't have any food, water, or pack but figured he was in pretty good shape and didn't really need anything. Maybe stop for breakfast somewhere first. He walked through the trees and past the B&B toward his car.

"Hello." Lafleur sat on the upstairs deck with his feet on a railing, holding a mug. "You want coffee?"

"Sure."

"Go in the kitchen and help yourself. It's on the stove."

Kirkland went in, leaving the sleeping bag by the door, found a mug in one of the cupboards, poured coffee from the old metal percolator warming on the stovetop, then rummaged in their refrigerator and found some milk to add. He went out and up the stairs, joining Lafleur.

"Another day in paradise," Kirkland said.

"How do we do it?" Lafleur replied. He gazed at the horizon, where the sun was starting to present itself. "It's going to be hot today. Perfect day to be on the river. You want to come?"

"Are you serious?"

"Yes. I have an open seat in my raft. Unless someone unexpected shows up."

"I'm kind of broke at the moment."

"Tell you what, Jack. You can come with us down to the diner in North River, have breakfast, and if there's still an open seat, you can have it. If another paying client comes, you're out of luck. But it's going to be a great day on the river. I can feel it. Of course, they're all great days. It's the nature of what we do."

"I'd love to."

"All right then."

"Alison's not coming?"

"No. She's sleeping in. Tell you what, though. I'll let you help me with the paperwork. You're an insurance guy, so it's right up your alley. Then you can listen to the safety briefing, which is pretty standard, and you'll see what this river is really like. And you'll see exactly the place where Jeanie Jones fell out, and the place she got hung up. That strainer's still there."

"That'd be great."

"I have a feeling that you're not only going to have a great day, you're going to learn what this is all about. I think you're going to have the same question I did about what happened. And I think you're going to come to the same conclusion."

"What's that?" Kirkland said.

"I don't want to lead you all the way to it. I think it's best if you just see, and figure it out for yourself."

Lafleur checked his boat and checked the equipment in the van, the life vests, helmets, paddles, and wetsuits. He went inside and came out dressed in shorts, Tevas, sunglasses that gripped his head tight, and a long-sleeve shirt of blue synthetic fleece over a T-shirt. They left before 8 a.m.

Kirkland drove behind the pickup truck and trailered raft. An hour and fifteen minutes later, they reached the diner. They took a table by the window and ordered eggs, toast, hash browns, and coffee. Before he could take a bite, Lafleur's clients showed up, two families with four adults and three adolescent girls, who pushed two adjacent tables together. He greeted each one and learned their names, explained how the day would go, and gave them all liability waivers, explaining that the parents needed to read them, fill them out correctly, and sign one for each person, including the children for whom they were responsible. He told them to give the forms to Jack when they were done, and told Jack to make sure they were all filled out correctly and signed and understood.

"I'd say you're in," he added.

Lafleur then ate his breakfast cold. The forms were essentially the same as those Kirkland had seen at the other company. He signed one as well, rereading the warning that rafting carried a risk of injury or death. Afterward, they drove several miles to the village of Indian Lake and turned down a back road that led to a big dirt parking area that was already filling up with cars, rafts on trailers, a couple of old school buses, and dozens of people stripping down to swimsuits, pulling on life vests, and unloading rafts. Wallace had his group unload the red raft and gather around it. As he began the safety talk, Alison pulled in with the van and approached the group.

"Right on time," he said. He introduced her and then resumed his talk. "First, let's get everyone set up with a flotation vest," he said. "They need to be comfortable because you wear them the whole time. They never come off. And they need to be snug."

Alison and Wallace made sure they were all buckled correctly. Then they tested them for looseness, and pulled tight the straps if necessary. They handed out helmets and checked the chin straps. They also offered wetsuit tops and bottoms. Lafleur said the water was about seventy degrees, and by early afternoon the air would be near eighty degrees, so they'd probably be okay without them. But it was their choice. The girls made faces at the old wetsuits, and everyone declined, even Kirkland, who was wearing jeans. Lafleur handed out paddles and gathered everyone again. He instructed them not to stand up in the river if they fell out but to lie back with their feet up. The danger, he said, lay in getting their feet stuck among the rocks while being under by the current. Rather than swim to shore, he said, they should stay in the main channel, hold onto the paddle, and by all means avoid downed trees. Just recently, he added, a woman got tangled in some branches and drowned.

"So stay near the boat if you can," he said. "Someone will pull you back in by the shoulders of your life vest." He demonstrated by stepping into the raft, reaching out, and sweeping one girl in after him. He also demonstrated how to throw the bag with the rescue rope in it. He promised to get everyone back. He repeated everything twice.

"You will float," Wallace said. "And if you come to a rock, you can push off it with your feet."

They offered everyone wetsuit booties to keep their feet warm. Water would collect in the bottom of the raft, and their feet would get wet. Guaranteed. And it would be fun. Guaranteed. Wallace drilled everyone on the paddling commands, showed them how to place their feet under the thwarts or tubes in front of them, how to sit for balance while leaning over the sides, and how to hold on when he yelled to hold on.

After stowing dry clothes in Alison's van, they surrounded the raft, picked it up on Lafleur's command, and carried it toward the water's edge, getting in line behind a dozen other rafts. There were two boats from Whitewater Big Time, the company Kirkland was investigating. Earlier he eavesdropped on their guides as they gave their instructions, and he noted that their customers seemed to be well equipped and prepared.

The trip did prove fun. The girls and their parents bounced, got wet, and laughed and shrieked often. In a stretch of flatwater, with the sun high and hot, Lafleur let the families swim in their life vests. When paddling, they synchronized their strokes according to the commands and rode through the rapids with little danger of tipping over. In three places, Lafleur yelled to hold on, and they did, as the raft bucked and dropped especially hard. At the Bus Stop, Wallace steered the raft along the edge of the hydraulic, close enough to feel the pull, and pointed out the tree to Jack.

"That's where she drowned," he said.

Kirkland stopped paddling and watched the current running under the tree. "How did she get way over there?" he said.

"That's a very good question," Wallace replied.

"She must have swam over there."

"Unless the current flowed sideways that day. And I'm pretty sure it didn't."

31

Kirkland helped load the raft and collect the gear, then ate the equivalent of three lunches, having missed dinner the night before. He was still grazing when the families were long finished, the girls lying in the sunshine, their parents chatting at the picnic table while Alison packed up. After securing the raft, Wallace made himself a sandwich and took it to the truck's cab, where he checked the payment receipts on the clipboard.

"I don't think we can afford to feed you," Alison said.

"You'd think I never ate before." Jack took another oatmeal cookie and kept chewing.

"I'd think you never did anything else."

"Now that's funny."

She laughed. "It is, actually. Kind of funny."

"And is this what you do as a trained psychologist? Put on buffet lunches?"

"I didn't finish my training."

"Why not continue?" Jack said. "Aren't you going to go back?"

"You ask a lot of questions."

"That's what I do." He looked at the river, wide and shallow, flowing quickly over the rocks. "I guess if you belonged in a place like this it wouldn't matter what you did. As long as you had a way to be here."

"I guess you're right." She kept packing up the food. Kirkland helped and didn't ask any more questions until Wallace appeared and said it was time to take him and the other two drivers back up to their cars at the put-in.

"Hey," Alison said. "I almost forgot to tell you something. It's about your case."

"What's that?"

"After we were done giving CPR, those other guys in her raft showed up. She was dead. And one of them said, 'Look what you did.'"

"Really? What does that mean?"

"I have no idea," Alison said. "I thought probably the trip was his idea, or something like that. But you said it was her idea."

"It was, according to everything I've been told. Which one said it?"

"I don't know. I don't know them. And at the time, I was on my knees over to the side, trying not to vomit. I didn't look up except to see the group of them come through the woods."

"What was the response? What did the other guy say back?"

"'I did not.' Something like that. 'Shut up.'"

"I don't think I'm done asking questions," Jack said.

Lafleur said he didn't hear that comment or anything like it. He was probably talking with the other guides then, deciding what to do. He doubted whether one of them said it to Randy, the guide whose raft she fell out of. He said it was unlikely Randy would have told anyone to shut up at that point, or ever.

Kirkland decided to ask everybody who was there.

32

Wilson Art & Design had declined to give him the home phone numbers and addresses of the four artists, but he got that information from the accident reports. In a notebook, he wrote down the name of each of them on a blank page, along with a brief description of what the artist had said in the first interview. He left plenty of space for everything he'd get with follow-up calls. Three lived in New York City. The fourth, the older one, Maloney, lived with his wife and children in New Jersey. Working from the office in Albany, Kirkland secretly recorded all the interviews, which might have been illegal on the interstate call. But he wasn't too worried about that. It was the only way to get down exactly what they said, and he was pretty sure that would be important in helping determine who was lying.

Jack was pretty sure the kid wasn't to blame, and neither was the company. He believed Jeanie Jones swam straight into her own fatal end, but she'd been given a big push in that direction. He figured she came up out of the hydraulic dazed and disoriented, maybe with a lungful of water already, panicked, and tried for the nearest shore. She got stuck in a strainer and drowned. Nobody helped her until Alison got there, too late. Don't grow old, Kirkland told himself, when nobody's got your back.

He called all the artists on the same weeknight, in quick succession, with the same questions, which he'd written out. He wanted the surprise. He reached Maloney first, after a child answered the phone, and told him he had some follow-up questions. Maloney only grunted.

"When you saw Jeanie Jones was lying there dead by the river, what did your co-worker mean when he said, 'Look what you did'?"

"I don't know what you're talking about," Maloney said.

"You didn't hear that?"

"No."

"Who said it?"

"I don't know."

"Why did he say it?"

"I told you I don't know."

"Was there anybody in the raft who wanted to see Jeanie Jones hurt?"

"I don't know anything about that," Maloney said.

"What I'm going to do next is schedule you for what's called an examination under oath. You can bring your lawyer. It's a legal examination. If you say anything untrue there, you can be prosecuted for criminal fraud." Kirkland gave that a moment to settle in. Then he gave Maloney his phone number and told him to call if he remembered something else. Otherwise, Kirkland would be in touch.

Playing back the answers, they seemed significant to him. Maloney didn't repeat that nobody had made the damning comment. Also he didn't flat-out deny that somebody wanted to see the woman hurt.

White, the tall one with the high forehead, answered the phone himself. He sounded genuinely baffled by the questions except the last one. "I don't think anybody liked her that much," he said, "but I don't think anybody would hurt her on purpose."

Reynolds, the short one with the mustache, denied everything. "That's crazy," he said. "I didn't hear anything."

When Kirkland phoned Van Peltz, the artist who'd doodled the whole time in the interview, the line was busy. He finally got through after a half-hour. He figured somebody had called Van Peltz to give him a heads-up. His guess was Reynolds. The two had walked in and out of the conference room together. Also, Kirkland had talked to Randy again, and the kid said he recalled the comment and was pretty sure Van Peltz had said it to Reynolds. Randy added that Reynolds made wisecracks to Jeanie Jones all that day—such as, "Why don't you fall out here, Jeanie? That would be fun."

So when he did get Van Peltz on the phone, Kirkland modified the questions.

"When you saw Jeanie Jones dead by the river, what did you mean when you said to Reynolds, 'Look what you did'?"

"I didn't mean anything."

"But you said it."

Silence. Jack continued: "Two people swear they heard you say it. I know, too, that none of you guys wanted to be there. It was her idea. Nobody liked her. And Reynolds was mocking her all day. And he was sitting right behind her when all three of you fell out. Those are the facts. And from the rafters I talked to, including the one in your raft, Reynolds shouldn't have fallen out. He had his feet under the thwart and a rope to grab on to, and it was only the bow that got sucked down to vertical. So what happened?"

"I don't know. You have to ask him."

"I did. I think he's lying about it. So I'm asking you. Also, you should be really clear about this. I'm going to schedule for you an examination under oath. And if you lie to me then, my company's going to give your name to the district attorney and recommend prosecution for fraud. But long before that, I'm going to call the trooper and the rangers you guys talked to and tell them you were lying to them. That means an obstruction charge for you and your friend and maybe the other two as well. And it also means a homicide investigation, with you as an accomplice."

"What?"

Jack had written out that little speech as well, after thinking through the possibilities. He figured Reynolds wouldn't say a word, suspecting how much trouble he might be in. But Van Peltz hadn't really done anything wrong, except decline to implicate his friend.

"Did he mean to kill her?"

"Are you out of your mind? Of course not."

"Then why did he fall on her?"

"He just wanted to make sure she fell in. She was bragging about it so much. How much fun it was."

"So he knocked her out of the boat."

"We all fell out. But he was on top of us. And then the raft was on top of him. And the water was sucking us down. Then the raft went by, and I popped up. And Lee was right there. We went downstream in the current like we were supposed to. I think Jeanie popped up after that."

33

On Tuesday evenings Lafleur went to yoga with a private teacher in Lake Placid. Alison declined to try it and had no immediate feeling for the lissome instructor, whom Wallace had introduced to her to one night in town. Instead, on the Tuesday evenings in late July and early August she pulled from her duffel bag the used copy of *Principles of Psychology* she'd picked up at the Lake Placid bookstore. She wanted to refresh her knowledge. Though she had been up north only three months, she was afraid she would start to forget some of those things she'd worked so hard to acquire. Besides, she found James fascinating. The book was dated but still foundational. He was fundamentally right about analysis, the logical criticism of views of the mind, and about introspection, something she hadn't done much of lately. Rereading James's best passages, she hoped to find some insight into everything that was going on her life—without that man present as an enormous though pleasurable distraction.

Summer was coming to a close. She could feel it in the morning chill. And yet this was the most prized part of the season. The days were warm, sunny, and perfect. The mosquitoes were gone. Wallace said soon they might see the Northern Lights at night, like he did last year. Alison lay on the bunk with the windows open, with the book next to her, and drifted, smiling. She thought of the Gaugin painting. *Where Do We Come From? What Are We? Where Are We Going?* She didn't know. And it was fine.

She was nearly asleep when she heard the screen door slam in the main part of the house. It was 8:36 p.m. on the clock and dark outside. Lafleur wasn't due back yet, and she hadn't heard the truck. It wasn't him. He would have looked in on her first, and he never let that door slap shut. She considered other possibilities, including his friends and his ex, but the one that seemed the most likely, and the most frightening, was Will. She'd quit expecting him to turn up again and suddenly thought that was naive. She gently lowered herself from the loft to the floor. She listened, then moved quickly to the door, opened it silently, slipped out and closed it, listened again, then walked barefoot over the grass and the dirt drive to the side door. Wallace's truck was nowhere in sight. She peeked in the mudroom, which was lit by one low-watt bulb. She didn't see anyone, but then she heard faint footfalls in the kitchen. The door to the kitchen was open.

She slipped into the mudroom and stepped quickly into an adjacent storage area where she kept her bow. She took it down from the wall, strung it, and pulled an arrow from the quiver Wallace had made her. She gripped the bow in her left hand, nocked an arrow on the bowstring with her right, and took a deep breath.

"You're going to be really sorry," she said softly. She raised the bow and crossed the mudroom in five long, silent steps and pointed the arrow into the kitchen, holding it in her drawn bow. Apart from a soft light coming from the oven, which she'd left open to cool after baking muffins, the room was dark. At the far end and to the right were doorways to other rooms. She didn't see anyone. A rectangular island stood in the center of the kitchen. Whoever it was could be crouched behind it. She tried to slow her breathing and steady her hands. She stepped to the left, softly, and thought of herself as Artemis or, better yet, Lottie. She took one more step, pulled the bowstring back in a full draw, and aimed the arrow.

The raccoon was big, nearly the size of a dog. It regarded her like it was uncertain, looked at the oven, then turned and waddled across the hardwood floor, past the island and through the mudroom. It pushed open the screen door and left, taking its time. Alison relaxed her grip on the bowstring, walked to the screen door, and latched it. She put the bow and arrow back, returned to the kitchen, and while still in the half-dark removed two dozen muffins from the muffin tins and put them in a basket, covering them with a checked cloth. She scrubbed the pans in the sink and dried them. When Wallace pulled in she was sitting in a chair in their bedroom, under a bright lamp, with the book open on her lap.

"What are you reading?" he said.

"Psychology."

"I see."

"How was class?"

"Blissful."

"I nearly shot a raccoon in your kitchen." Alison was matter of fact.

"Really? Is Hubert back?"

"Hubert?"

"The world's largest raccoon. He used to visit sometimes. I haven't seen him in a while."

"He was really big. I thought he was a man, at first. Anyway, he may not be back right away. I think he knew I was serious."

"Did you put the shotgun on him?"

"No. Just my bow. With an arrow. I had it drawn. I was just about to let it fly when he looked at me."

"Then I think Hubert was wise to leave," Wallace said.

"Yes. Yes, he was."

"And I probably don't have to worry at all about leaving you home alone."

"No," Alison said. "No, you don't."

"And if it had been a couple of big ugly guys from Long Island ..."

"One of them would still be trying to get the arrow out," Alison said.

34

The next afternoon, following another rafting trip where she drove the van and put on lunch, Alison got a ride to Newcomb and canoed down to Lottie's. She found her aunt sitting at her typewriter in the sunshine outside the cabin. She was wearing a black swimsuit, her silver hair tied up behind her head. The woman looked half her age and smiled broadly as the dogs barked and bounded out to greet her niece. Alison bent low, and the dogs nuzzled and licked her face.

"That's enough," Lottie said. But Alison dropped her bag and reached her arms around them, and they nuzzled her some more. "Are you moving back?"

"For a few days. I missed you."

"Did you now? Well, I want you to know it's good to see you, too." Lottie stood and walked around the table and hugged her. She stepped back and looked her over. "You're different."

"Since you saw me last week?"

"Mmm, hmmm. Since then. And especially since that poor bedraggled thing I found at the train station. Well, come in. Bring your bag. Your room is waiting, as always."

They chatted for an hour about Lottie's bird reports and ate pasta by candlelight, then sat out sipping tea and looking at the stars.

"How did you know you wanted to be a scientist?"

"I just always did," Lottie said. "Ever since I was a little girl. Though I didn't have the name for it then. Your grandmother said I should have been a boy. I was always outside and bringing things home, like birds' eggs and salamanders. Your grandmother did not like that. Now, your mother, she had dolls. Beautiful ones with lovely clothes and real hair you could brush."

"She was younger."

"She still is. But don't tell her I said so. She doesn't like to be reminded."

"Did you like school?" Alison held the warm mug to her face and sipped.

"Oh, yes. When I got to the university there weren't a lot of women doing what I was doing. I was the only one in a lot of my classes. But I couldn't have imagined doing anything else. And so I stayed until I was done. I wanted that Ph.D."

"You did your doctoral research in South America?"

"I did."

"Then how did you end up here?"

"One summer I worked at an inn. That was on Fourth Lake. And I married the owner."

"You what?" Alison was surprised she hadn't heard that story.

"It didn't work out. So I went back and finished my degree. But I got research work here and found that I didn't really want to be anyplace else. So I stayed."

"It's that simple."

"It usually is. I didn't want anybody telling me what to do. And I didn't have to. It's good to get an education." Lottie looked pointedly at Alison.

"I'm getting my guide's license in a few days. I'm going down to Albany to take the written test. And I've still got first-aid and CPR certifications. And now I have the required five rafting trips."

"Was this his idea?" Lottie said.

"He thought it would be good in case I ever want to guide on my own," Alison said. "It's something to have. It's good for five years."

"So you see yourself as a river guide?"

"For now. Maybe later I'll start a unique practice, river psychotherapy."

"Isn't that what your boyfriend says he does?"

"He does." Alison laughed. "And it works in a certain way. I think I could add something a little more grounded in academic theory and clinical practice."

For the next few days, Alison hunted with the dogs. She revisited all the blinds and tree stands she'd used as a girl and sat quietly with the dogs and held her bow, watching for wildlife. She walked through the forest with them trotting ahead and flushing out squirrels and birds. The dogs had been trained, and they stopped and pointed and on her command chased the animals into the open. She practiced sighting on them but didn't shoot an arrow.

She had no intention of hurting any of them. She also went still hunting by herself, leaving the dogs in the cabin, trying to move slowly and silently, then standing as still as any predator, with an arrow nocked and ready.

Alison was thinking of joining Wallace in guiding hunters in the autumn deer season, at least the early part that was bow season. He took hunters out in bear season, too, even though he considered the bear his spirit animal. He'd talked several hunters out of taking a shot, urging them to just appreciate the contact and experience. Deer season was something else. They were food. She'd read a biologist's theory that they were hard-wired as prey, thrilled by the chase. Wallace said that made sense and that good hunters tried to see things as well as they could from the prey's perspective, always regarding the deer with respect and gratitude. Alison still didn't think she wanted to kill anything, though she liked the pursuit.

35

Kirkland phoned Lafleur twice more after interviewing the artists and shared what he'd learned. He said he was planning to call the State Police and the rangers.

"There will be consequences to that," Wallace said.

"Sure, but they might not be that bad. One guy fooled around in a kind of mean-spirited way, with obviously tragic consequences, and they told some lies by omission. This kind of thing happens, especially with car accidents. Somebody's speeding, or drinking, or racing, and somebody winds up seriously injured or dead. And nobody volunteers the truth."

"I don't know whether you've been paying attention lately, but a lot of those bad DWIs, they're going to prison. It's the eighties, and there's very little tolerance in some circles for what used to pass for high jinks. Zero tolerance. You've heard the phrase."

"What do you think I should do?"

"I think you should do the right thing," Wallace said. "And that's your conscience."

"Not completely. My boss says I have to contact the police. He's already called the lawyer for the design company and told him what we found out and said they should withdraw the claim. I think he wants the police involved. That would put the whole thing beyond question. In any event, he says I have knowledge of a crime and it's my obligation to share it."

"Alison will be glad you did. She took this thing to heart. She thinks the woman was treated badly. Hard to argue with that."

"Talking to her, she seems to be quite the feminist," Jack said. "She also doesn't seem to like men very much. Or at least she doesn't seem to like me."

"I think in her experience some men are dogs. I take that back. She has a higher opinion of dogs than that." Wallace laughed. "She has a point."

"Not all men."

"I would say not all, but I'm not exactly impartial. She does believe that women have the right to fight back. And since this woman couldn't, it was important to her that you were doing it. That someone was doing it."

The next morning, Kirkland contacted both the ranger captain and the troop major to discuss what he believed he knew. Within an hour he had callbacks from a police investigator and one of the rangers. Before the end of the day, it was a reopened police case, and despite his protests otherwise, the investigator called it a possible homicide investigation. Kirkland declined to give him his files or the artists' contact information without a warrant or court order, saying it was proprietary information belonging to his agency.

"You don't want to do that," the police investigator said.

Kirkland put him on hold, found the name of a lawyer the agency used, and gave that name to the policeman if he wanted to pursue it that way. "You should have their contact information somewhere in your reports. I think you'll scare them a lot easier than you'll scare me."

He called Lafleur again to warn him this thing might get crazy and to warn Alison, though he'd made a point not to drop either of their names, and he wanted Wallace to know that.

"I appreciate that," Lafleur said. "I think she will too."

When Alison returned from Albany that evening, having borrowed her aunt's truck, she pulled into the B&B's driveway and Wallace came out to meet her. They hadn't seen each other for several days, and neither could stop smiling. Alison threw her arms around him and pressed against the sturdy contours of his body. She pulled back her head and kissed him for a long time. He wrapped his arms around her waist. He kissed her back. She shifted, pressing her hips into him, and leaned back.

"I can't stay," Alison said.

"Why not?"

"There's a letter at my aunt's cabin. It's from the university. My mother forwarded it two weeks ago. I called her today, and she told me. I guess Lottie forgot to mention it when I was there. It might be time-sensitive. Anyway, I need to see it and figure out what to do about it. I also have to return her truck."

"I can follow you down, canoe down with you, and we can come back tonight."

"It's late. And you've got a trip tomorrow," Alison said. "Has Donny been doing okay with the van and the lunches?"

"He's not you. But, yes, he's doing all right."

"Good."

"How was the licensing test?"

"Easy. I'm sure I passed." She kissed him quickly on the mouth, cupped his lips with her hand, kissed him again, and stepped away. "I'll be back tomorrow. And If I can't for any reason, I'll call you."

"Right," Wallace said. He tried to conceal how let down he felt.

After watching her drive off, Lafleur went inside and half-filled a bucket with hot water and soap, grabbed a scrub brush and big sponge, and began cleaning. He scrubbed both bathrooms—the floors, sinks, toilets, and tubs, which had gotten little more than cursory wipe-downs since the summer guests started arriving in June. He changed the bucket water, cleaned the brush and sponge, and then scoured the kitchen as well. He cleaned the stovetop and burners and the oven and slid the appliances out to clean behind them on the walls and floor. He got on his knees and scrubbed the entire floor. Alison had been keeping on top of the laundry, but he washed a load of towels and found one of her shirts and a flannel nightgown.

He worked until nearly midnight, trying not to think too much. Then he checked the truck, trailer, and rafting gear, made sure the keys were in the van, and reminded himself to phone Donny in the morning to let him know that he needed him again. He thought of telling him he might need him for the rest of the summer, or some part of it, but that seemed like bad luck. He slept soundly on his own unlaundered sheets, which still had Alison's scent. He woke in the morning with determined optimism, chatted up his clients at the diner, and approached the river like he was seeing it again for the first time.

"How do we do it?" he shouted after they came out of the first rapids, wet and smiling. When they passed Virgin Falls he didn't tell that story, even though his clients were incoming college freshmen who probably would have liked it.

36

Charlotte Delos knew by its heft and the return address what was in the large envelope. Not that much had changed since her university days. Simple notices and rejections were thin envelopes. Applications and registration packets were fat. She debated whether to take it in her truck to Lafleur's place and hand it to Alison. The postmark was ten days old. She decided against it, bought a few things at the store, and went home in the boat. The thing about universities, which she knew firsthand, was they moved slowly and doctoral students didn't get treated like undergraduates. There were relatively few of them, and it wasn't easy to get chosen, certainly not in the good programs. They breathed some of the same rarefied air as professors, who tended to regard them more as future colleagues than annoyances. The academy had many researchers and administrators who had surpassed their teachers. Abuse those coming up at your own risk.

Alison's deadlines could slip, seeing she had been selected, Lottie was fairly certain. And the girl needed to decide without interference which world she wanted. Lottie herself had left her studies for two years to help run an inn. But it was the forest and wildlife she didn't want to leave, not really the innkeeper or the guests who wanted to be waited on. She liked the rigors of science and was patient, industrious, thorough, intrigued. The terminal degree guaranteed her respect from those who didn't have one, and it made her a peer of those who did. The hard sciences were meritocracies. Make your research sound, and let your critics pound sand. So she went back and earned the credential and got published and kept going.

Her niece had a similar feeling for the wilderness. That had been clear when she was young. Lottie had often wondered why the girl never accepted her invitations to visit in the summer. She wasn't exactly surprised when she learned that Alison's mother hadn't shared the invitations. Now Alison's mother had forwarded the registration packet. This felt somewhat the same, and Lottie acknowledged that might be part of the reason she didn't tell Alison about it right away. Also, she liked having her niece around, even if she were spending most nights in Lake Placid. She wondered if she should have had a daughter of her own but quickly dismissed the thought. Lottie had no time for remorse and little for introspection. It was too bad, though, that Alison wasn't interested in the natural sciences. There was plenty to keep a scientist busy in the Adirondack Park. Almost half of its six million acres was protected by the state constitution as Forest Preserve ("which shall be forever kept as wild forest lands"). Lottie was doing whatever she could, along with a lot of other committed people, to make sure that it remained so. Even Lafleur, she grudgingly admitted, took up the cause when he fought against the aerial spraying of insecticides. He wasn't a bad sort. A little loopy. But he was better than a lot of men.

When Alison returned to the cabin that evening, she immediately asked for the mail.

"It's right there. It's the big one with your name on it."

Alison picked it up, felt it, and looked at the addresses. She set it down again.

"It looks like they still want you."

"I hadn't been thinking about it. I'm not really ready for this. I just took the guide's test today."

"If nothing else," Lottie said, "you should talk to them."

"I actually had a dream about it several nights ago. My adviser was in it. He was talking about something. I couldn't hear him, or I can't recall. It seemed unimportant until now."

"Hmmm."

"That's what the subconscious does," Alison said. "It keeps track of all the crap you're trying to forget."

They had dinner and talked about other things. Afterward Alison opened the envelope and confirmed that she had been accepted.

"I guess the question is what you want to do at this juncture for your career," Lottie said. "What your priorities are. Or your preferences."

"I always thought I could have been a good thief. I'm also an excellent forger."

"I don't think I care to know how you know that," Lottie said.

"The last paper I wrote was about a man who had come in for a clinical evaluation. My adviser was doing the evaluation. This man agreed to let some students sit in. There was testing and an interview. He had a terrible past, a really horrible childhood, and he had cognitive and behavioral issues, I don't even recall them all. So in my final paper, about his diagnosis and what to do to help him, I wrote that he deserved to catch a break and should go back and get decent parents, in a special deal with whoever runs the universe. It was my last paper. I was sure I failed."

"I guess," Lottie said, "that somehow you must have passed."

37

The next morning, Alison left a long phone message for Wallace telling him she wouldn't return for a day or two, that she had to go back down to the university and talk to some people to make arrangements about school. They had kept her place in the Ph.D. program, which included the teaching assistant's position and stipend, but they'd wanted a reply by August 15. The deadline had passed. She thought it was too late for this year, she said, but wanted to talk to them about next year or the year after, and she needed to do it in person. She'd call again as soon as she knew something. Meantime, could he keep finding someone to fill in? She left Lottie's truck at the Rensselaer station and took an afternoon train to the city, then the Long Island Rail Road out to Cold Spring Harbor, where her mother picked her up.

"You look well," Dolores said. She added, "You need to do something about your hair. It looks like Lottie's. It's all over the place."

"You haven't seen her in a decade, not since I graduated from high school. How would you know?"

"I see her photograph in the back of her books. You'd think she could afford to go to the hairdresser once in a blue moon."

"Well, she sends her little sister her regards," Alison said, watching to see if that pushed any buttons. But Dolores had on her game face. It was impossible to tell.

"Does she now? Well, that's nice."

They rode in silence until they reached the narrow road that led to the house. A small, tasteful real-estate sign stood at the end of the road, with another at the edge of the property's eight acres.

"You're selling the house?"

"Oh, no. I sold it already. They won't take the signs down yet, though, not until all the contingencies are satisfied and the closing is scheduled."

"You weren't going to tell me?"

"I just did. This all happened very recently. I can't afford it anymore. And it's a good price."

"What are you going to do?"

"I've found a little place in Connecticut near your sister," Dolores said, slowing the Lincoln to a stop by the front door. "And what are your plans?"

"I'll find out tomorrow," Alison said. "I have a meeting with the department chair."

While her mother watched the news and heated a frozen dinner for them, Alison walked the property. She admired the size and age of the trees and smelled the air in a way she hadn't before. She walked barefoot across her father's lawn, felt the lush grass, admired her mother's rosebushes and hydrangeas (now tended again), and thought her parents had been on to something. The best private piece of nature their money could buy close to the city.

In the morning, she borrowed her mother's car, and after an hour with the professor who'd been evolving into her mentor and the other one who chaired the psychology department, she had an agreement for returning. She went home and told her mother and decided to stay one more night, probably the last one in the house where she'd spent so many years. She didn't call Wallace, who would have been in and out getting ready for the next rafting trip. She wanted to see him when she told him. She did phone the police investigator on the drowning case and confirmed what she'd heard the artists say. What had happened in Kirkland's investigation had made her furious. The trooper told her he was having the artists questioned by an investigator in the city. She also called and berated Kirkland for refusing to share more information with the police.

"That's their job," he said.

"Dull normal," she said. Before she hung up, he told her the police thought they'd eventually give the case to the district attorney, who would take it to a grand jury.

"What does that mean?"

"They say a grand jury will indict a stump if the DA asks them to. The defense isn't represented at all. So I'm guessing at least one or two of them will get charged with something."

The next morning her mother drove her back to the Cold Spring Harbor train station, where Alison boarded among a few well-heeled commuters, none of whom she recognized.

"Come back soon," Dolores said. "And do something about your hair before you do."

"You won't be here."

"Well, you know what I mean. In Connecticut. You don't see your sister enough."

She caught the Amtrak train north out of Penn Station, which looked less seedy with a crowd in it. She saw Storm King Mountain this time and the fortress that was West Point, and she thought her river didn't look too bad. There were many small sailboats on the water below the military academy, sleek and quick, and at Kingston she saw three individual rowers sculling smoothly on the glassy river.

At the Rensselaer station, she got in the pickup truck, crossed the bridge, and drove north on the interstate to the Newcomb exit and followed the two-lane to the general store. There were hints of burgundy and yellow in a few of the distressed trees near the road. From the pay phone, she left a message for Wallace, who was back on the river, that she'd see him the next morning and wanted to ask him something. She canoed down to Lottie's and that evening shared all her news. Lottie had some of her own. She was putting her farm up for sale. Nobody had been charged with the arson there. The investigation hadn't gone anywhere. She decided not to go back. She was planning on winterizing the cabin and bringing in a big supply of firewood.

38

Will and George borrowed an old rowboat with a twelve-horsepower outboard and trailered it all the way from Long Island to Newcomb. They backed it into the Hudson shortly after 11 p.m., a few hours behind Alison. A friend had seen her in Huntington pumping gas into the old Lincoln at the self-service station and told Will. He got a woman he knew from work to phone the house. Alison was already gone, but the woman told Dolores she was a friend and was trying to get in touch and had seen Alison but had no idea where she'd gone. Dolores told her what she knew: Lottie's name, where she lived, the phone number at the general store, and the number of the pay phone outside. She also told her that Alison had been working as a rafting guide but was planning to come back and go to school. Will already knew most of this, but he now had fairly specific directions to the cabin. He also thought he might have figured in her plans to return to Long Island.

At the Northway rest stop on the way up to the mountains, Will leafed through the glossy state travel guide and the Adirondack brochures and found the ad for Lafleur's B&B and rafting company. He and George were pretty sure the smiling bearded character in the pamphlet was their pizza man. They took two copies of the brochure, checked the address, and checked its approximate location on the map. They decided he'd be their last stop, probably around first light when he'd be sleepy and not too suspicious.

"Long Island rules," Will said.

"Nobody moves and somebody gets hurt," George replied.

Their plan, more or less, was to knock on his door and surprise him like he'd surprised them. See how he liked it. Will would hold his .38 on him while George beat the shit out of him. Then they'd drive home with Alison. He'd worked out what he was going to say. That this was the right thing to do. That he forgave her. It was time for her to forgive him. It was time for her to be a little less emotional. That was really the problem. That she was a little too emotional. He'd remind her what she said, that they'd work it out. It was time for her to keep her word and come back and work it out. He was sure she'd agree. He believed she felt the same way he did. Before leaving the rest stop, George called Lafleur's business phone. Wallace answered as he always did, asking in a cheerful voice what he could do for the caller.

"That's him," George whispered to his brother. Then he hung up.

In Newcomb, after sliding the boat in the water, Will parked the pickup up the road a bit, toward the general store. George got into the boat, and Will pushed off and jumped in. George primed and started the small engine.

"How will we find this place?" he said.

"It's about a mile down. After the river gets narrow. The guy said you can see a path on the left and there's a cabin back through the trees. There should be a canoe and a skiff by the shore and a no-trespassing sign."

"What if the old lady's difficult? You said she's got guns."

"That's what I heard. She's got shotguns. So what? I don't think it's a problem. Alison will straighten her out. And if she pulls any kind of shit I've got my gun."

"Showdown with an old lady," George said. "That's classic."

"You can wrestle her to the ground," Will replied. "You haven't had a girlfriend in a long time."

"You're about as funny as Jackie Mason."

The first call had woken Lafleur and put him slightly on edge. It may have been unimportant, just a hang-up call, but he was unsettled by the muffled voice in the background. The caller had not been alone. The second call, an hour later from Rita, who stayed the summer in a trailer behind the general store, sent him out the door.

"I wasn't going to call you, but you said to if that guy ever came back or if there was anything real suspicious. I'm not saying it's him, but two guys in a little outboard just went down the river, and I know Alison's down there at Lottie's. There's a pickup truck and trailer out here that I don't recognize. It probably isn't anything. But I said I'd call, so I did. Bobby said not to. It's probably just fishermen getting an early start. But I never heard of fishing at midnight."

"Thank you, Rita. Is there a motorboat there I can borrow?"

"Not that I know of. Not tonight."

Lafleur took his pistol and car keys and went out in the shorts he was sleeping in. He detached his trailer from the truck, threw his canoe and one paddle in the truck bed, made sure the short rope was back there where he usually left it, and pulled out of the drive and headed down the two-lane highway, quickly reaching 80 mph, braking and slowing only for the tight turns. He nearly lost control of the truck twice, and once he almost hit an oncoming car. He knew he was at least a good hour behind and had a bad feeling.

The dogs were up and pacing, whining softly, which woke Lottie. She had once been a heavy sleeper, but since the arson she slept fitfully, even with Alison around. Lottie heard the boat engine. She didn't keep a clock but looked out the window at the sky and the crescent moon through the trees. The engine shut off. She heard two men's voices and through the trees saw the beam of a flashlight approaching.

"It's too late for visitors," she told Marx.

Lottie shushed the dogs and opened the door to the bedroom, where Alison was breathing softly. She knelt, pushed two baskets aside and slid the shotgun out from under the bed. She returned to the front room and pulled the bedroom door closed. She left the lights off. It was a break-action gun. She usually left the pump-action shotgun locked in the truck. That was where she expected the trouble, out in the world. Not here. Only a small group of people knew where the cabin was. Lottie opened the gun , inserted two shells, and closed it again. She flipped off the safety and peered out the curtained window next to the door. The voices grew louder. Their light shone on the outside of the cabin and around the edges of the curtain. One of the dogs barked.

"They've got a dog," George said. "Why didn't you know that?"

Will didn't reply and kept walking toward the cabin.

Alison shuffled out of the bedroom. "What's going on?"

"There's someone here," Lottie whispered. "Some men."

Their footfalls on the porch sent the dogs into a frenzy, barking and jumping at the window and door. Will tried to shine the light in the window. He couldn't see anyone inside, just the faces of the dogs when they managed briefly to push up under the curtain.

"There's two of them," he said. "I don't know if there's any people here."

Alison had moved into the corner, to Lottie's side, away from the sliver of the light beam. She could see at a sharp angle out the window. It was impossible to see the men clearly in the dark, but she immediately knew the voice. Too late, she touched Lottie's arm and whispered, "No." Her aunt didn't hear her. But Lottie had made up her own mind anyway.

Will knocked.

"What do you want?" Lottie shouted over the barking.

"We've come to see Alison."

"Who are you?"

"A friend."

"Hold on. I can't hear you."

Lottie pulled the cloth curtain more completely across the front window, then turned a lamp on. Alison retreated to the bedroom. She pulled on her Tevas. She grabbed her bow and quiver from the corner. Sitting on the bed, she pushed out the window screen with her feet. It was stapled in place on the inside. The wood shutters had been latched open on the outside to let in the night air.

Lottie pulled the dogs into the bedroom by their collars, then closed the door. She didn't notice Alison was halfway out. She held the shotgun across her chest with her right hand near the trigger and unlatched the front door with her left and opened it slightly.

Will stood on the threshold. She couldn't clearly see the other man behind him.

"Hello," he said. "I'm here to see Alison."

"It's late," Lottie said.

"I know. It was a long drive. And then that boat ride." His right hand held the .38 behind his back. He was worried about the dogs. Looking at the shotgun the diminutive woman now held in both hands, he said, "Here, please put the gun down before you hurt somebody."

"It's my gun," Lottie said. "Who's with you?"

"That's my brother, George," Will replied. "Come on in and introduce yourself."

Will started to step into the room. George followed. The dogs barked madly in the bedroom and scratched at the door. Lottie backed up two steps and bumped into a chair.

"Damn it," she said. "Quiet!"

The dogs stopped barking.

Will paused at the doorway.

"I just want to talk to Alison. I'm sure she'll want to see me. She can't be sleeping. Can you please ask her to come out?"

"Come back tomorrow," Lottie said. "In the daylight. I mean it. Not tonight. It's late."

"All right, all right. Don't get nervous. We're leaving." Will backed out onto the porch. "I don't know what's wrong with you people up here."

He backed into George, who took two steps back, then missed the single stair and fell off the porch. "Goddamn it!"

Will half turned. He nearly laughed. He stepped off the porch, crouched next to his brother, and held his shoulder down with one hand. "Now look what happened. I think he's hurt."

"He's what?" Lottie said. The dogs had started barking again.

"He's hurt," Will yelled. "Take a look."

Alison had stayed near the window, trying to listen. She hung the quiver over her head and shoulder and strung the bow. She called Marx and DaVinci to her, and they stopped barking and jumped on the bed, sniffing her. After hearing a brief struggle, followed by a thump, she slid out the window feet first. She reached in and held the dogs' collars and told them to be still. The moment the door opened, she saw Will.

"Get him!" she ordered in a harsh whisper.

Marx ran through the door first, DaVinci at his shoulder. They hit Will in the chest, knocking him over, and went for his throat. George, standing behind him, squeezed the trigger of the shotgun, the birdshot hitting high on the wall. The deafening blast failed to deter the dogs. When Will fell backwards to the floor, he dropped his handgun. Marx grabbed him by the throat firmly, but as if Will were a pheasant, without biting down and breaking the skin. DaVinci stood alert next to him.

"Kill him," Will croaked. Marx growled when the man moved.

Alison whistled. The dogs turned, ran into the bedroom, jumped on the bed, and one at a time jumped out the window, Marx right behind DaVinci. They followed Alison, who turned to run among the trees. She heard a second shotgun and sensed something whiz past over her shoulder. George must have sprayed the bedroom with birdshot in an attempt to shoot the dogs, but it flew too high. She had no doubt Lottie was hurt and feared she might even be dead. She ran twenty yards into the woods, the dogs at her heels at first, then running ahead. She stopped behind the thick sugar maple. When she was a girl, Alison had used a hollow among the roots as her first blind. From there she could watch the cabin unseen. The dogs came back to her.

She heard the men step out onto the deck.

"Why did you hit her so hard?" Will asked.

"She was going to shoot you."

"Christ." Will walked to the side of the cabin and called for Alison.

"Come back," he yelled. "Your aunt's hurt. She tried to shoot us."

Alison pulled an arrow from the quiver and nocked it on the bowstring. She had only four arrows. She tried to keep her voice calm and reasonable, the way she did when she'd talked Will into letting her go months ago.

"I think it would be best if you go now," she said. "So I can take care of her."

"You have to come with me," Will said, lowering his voice, realizing she wasn't far. He shined the light in her direction but didn't see her. "You promised you'd come back. It's time."

"I can't do that yet. Later, I think, it might be possible. But not like this. Tell me what you did to my aunt."

"I'm not going to wait four more months just to see you again. I think you know what's right. I think you know where you belong."

Alison heard the footsteps and saw George's silhouette coming around the cabin, approaching her from another direction, trying to be stealthy, following the sound of her voice. She crouched lower and whispered to the dogs to stay, then stood. She drew back the bowstring and aimed.

"I've got a gun. You've got to control those dogs or else I'm going to have to shoot them." Will shined the light into the woods, moving it back and forth, but he couldn't see her or the dogs.

"Call off your brother," Alison said.

George started running toward her voice. "She's right here," he said.

Then he screamed.

39

Alison had aimed for the kill zone. She was more furious than afraid. They must have hurt Lottie badly as she wasn't making a sound. But they didn't seem to care. They weren't going to back off. She felt she didn't have a choice when she shot George. The arrow hit high on the chest, near the shoulder. The field point pierced the muscle and hit the bone in the back of his shoulder. The scream started low and guttural, then went high and intermittent, like sobbing.

Will had heard the sound before, when they were kids and his brother went off a jump on a motorbike, landed sideways, and broke his leg. The bone was sticking out from his shin. When their mother died, Will was thirteen and George nine. The younger boy attached himself to his older brother. Their old man was always working and made Will be responsible. That was a pain in the ass sometimes because George was clumsy, kind of immature, especially for his size, and had a tendency to get in trouble.

"George!" Will came crashing through the woods with the flashlight and shined it on his brother, who began sobbing in earnest, only fifteen yards from Alison's maple tree. She lay the bow down and grabbed both growling dogs by their collars. "Stay," she said softly.

"Fucking kill her!" George shrieked. He resumed sobbing.

"Shit. There's an arrow sticking out of you." Will shined the light on him and looked closely at where it pinned the edges of George's shirt into the puncture wound. "It's not bleeding."

Alison released the dogs and picked up the bow, took another arrow from the quiver, and nocked it. "I'll shoot you, too, unless you leave now," she said.

Will turned and aimed the light toward her. He saw the dogs on either side of the tree, though not Alison. He knew she was right there, behind the tree.

She heard the yelp immediately after the first boom of the pistol, then another boom and yelp. Her ears ringing, she didn't hear him close the distance. He shined the light on one side of the maple. When she leaned in the other direction, he grabbed a handful of her hair and slammed her head against the trunk. Alison went to her knees. She dropped the bow and grabbed the arrow shaft in both hands and jammed the point into his thigh. Her hands slid down the shaft. It didn't go deep. Will spun away. Alison scrambled up and ran into the woods, zigzagging in case he shot at her. She didn't stop running for a hundred yards, then held up behind a yellow birch, caught her breath, and listened. She could hear their faint voices, still near the cabin.

It was a tree she had climbed as a girl, a low aerie from which she commanded this piece of the forest. She would perch herself on a limb about ten feet up where the tree had once split. It had grown in twelve years. She shinnied and scrambled up to the branch and stood hugging the trunk. She didn't think Will would look up. But it didn't begin to solve her problem. She thought about making her way in a big loop back to the river and going for help, except he'd hear her starting the boat engine. And the canoe would be too slow. They'd catch her. She was pretty sure the dogs were dead or soon would be. There was no whimpering. She wondered if Lottie was dead too. She thought about waiting it out. She knew she'd hit George with a good shot and they'd have to get him out of there for medical treatment. She decided to wait a bit. Then she'd climb down and stalk back slowly to her bow, as if she were hunting. She still had two arrows in the quiver.

After his encounter with Alison, Will pulled the arrow out of his thigh and cursed. It had gone in only an inch or two and came out easily. He picked up the flashlight, looked around, and found the pistol. He saw the bow and stepped on it hard. It didn't break. He threw it. He kicked both dogs and walked over to George, who was grunting and whimpering, and shined the light on him.

"That doesn't look too bad."

"How the fuck would you know."

"She stuck me in the leg with one of those. It's just a target arrow."

"Good for you, asshole."

"Here," Will said. "Let me pull it out."

"Don't touch it!"

"Then you pull it out."

"I can't. It's fucking agony. I need to go to the hospital."

"Don't be a baby," Will said. "Get up. I'll see if they've got some booze in the cabin. You can wait in the boat."

George cursed and resumed crying as he struggled to his feet. Will left him with the light, walked around the cabin, and went in the front door. He ignored Lottie, who was lying on the porch, blood pooled near her mouth. He opened all the cabinets and found a nearly full bottle of Jameson's. He walked out to find George stumbling by and tried to hand the bottle to him.

"I can't. I can't lift that arm." He sobbed harder.

"Fine. I'll walk you to the boat. You're such a fucking baby, I can't believe it."

"I hate you," George said. "I absolutely fucking hate you and this stupid idea. She's just some stupid girl. Now look what she's fucking done."

"I'll take care of it. Just sit there in the boat and drink. If you get shitfaced enough, I'll pull it out."

"Don't you touch it!" George said. He looked at the arrow sticking out of him and started sobbing again.

"Give me that light, you big baby."

Will's thigh began to throb. Alison had a lot to answer for. Not coming back as she had promised. That's where the problem started. The pizza man with the gun. The old woman who pulled the shotgun on them. Putting the dogs on him. She shot George with a fucking arrow. And she stuck him in the leg. It was time for an attitude adjustment. She didn't know what was for her own good. Women need to be told. He remembered the lines from an old movie.

"I'll beat you."

"How else will I know that you love me?"

Will figured he'd been too easy with Alison. He'd let her do whatever she wanted. And she just got deeper into trouble. Now it was time to take her home, whatever that required. After checking the cabin again, he returned to the tree where he found her and then began walking in the direction she had fled.

Alison stood in the tree, listening. Her face was tender, swollen around one eye. She felt the sore spots on her scalp and thought he'd probably pulled some hair out. Eventually, concern for Lottie compelled her to climb out of the tree. She slowly, carefully walked forty steps north before turning west back toward the cabin. She didn't want to be in Will's path if he came looking for her. When she got to the cabin, she peered in the windows and saw no one. She slipped around to the front and in the light from the open door saw Lottie lying by the wooden porch. Alison crouched beside her. She was breathing but unconscious. The side of her face was misshapen, and it looked like blood had flowed out of her mouth and nose. Evidently, George had struck her with the rock that lay near the body.

Alison went back into the woods and listened. The quiet was broken by George's shout from the river. "Hey, hurry the fuck up!"

Alison ran to the maple where she'd lost the bow. It wasn't there. She felt the dogs, both cold.

"Alison!" Will's voice carried through the trees. "It's time to talk. I'll stay all night. As long as it takes."

The flashlight was coming back. In the faint light of the crescent moon she groped around the ground for the bow but couldn't find it. She moved off when Will came nearer, circling away from the beam of light as it scanned the woods. When Will was thirty yards off, she heard his crunching footfalls. At twenty yards, his beam glinted off the fiberglass of the bow. After Will passed and entered the cabin, she hurried to the bow and picked it up. Then he came out again.

"Alison! You won't like what happens if you don't show yourself. I'm not going to hurt you. I just want to talk."

40

Lafleur stopped paddling upstream of the cabin and drifted with the current, steering the boat near the shore. He slowed his breathing and listened. He heard the sobbing first. Then shouting and Alison's name. The first, he thought, was a bad sign. Maybe Lottie was hurt. The second meant Alison was probably okay. He landed just above the usual takeout, got out quietly, and crept up the bank. Following the edge of the forest, he came upon George, lying in the front of the rowboat, tilting a bottle toward his big face. As Lafleur watched from above, George moved slightly, dropped the bottle, and put his free hand to his shoulder. When Lafleur saw the arrow, he was both delighted and alarmed.

"I said hurry the fuck up!" George bellowed.

Lafleur went back to the canoe for the rope. He made a slip knot, returned to the rowboat, and pushed his gun in George's face.

"Shhh," he said. "I'm going to tie you up now."

He holstered the gun, slipped the loop over George's free wrist, and pulled it tight. He looped the rope around George's other wrist, and yanked them together. He wrapped the wrists several time and knotted the rope.

George screamed.

Will ran to the edge of the woods. Against the river glistening softly in the pale light of the stars and slivered moonlight, he saw a man's silhouette near the boat. When the figure started moving quickly up the clearing toward him, Will gripped his pistol with both hands and aimed. He waited until he had a sure shot. He had no doubt who it was.

The arrow ricocheted off Will's skull, and he grunted as he fell. Alison had been waiting in the shadows near the clearing, knowing Will would pass by on his way to the boat. She had seen Lafleur approach and heard George's scream. When Will appeared and aimed his pistol, he was only twenty feet away. She shot her arrow at his head, just as she had practiced with the effigy. She let Lafleur get to him first.

"Nice shot," Wallace said when she reached him a moment later. The arrow left a nasty wound near the crown, under the hair. He wasn't moving. Wallace looked up at her. "Is there anybody else here?"

"Just Lottie. She's badly injured. I think they broke bones in her face. And they killed the dogs." Alison's hands were shaking. He tried to hug her. She pushed him away.

"How are you?"

"Good. I'm good," she said.

"I'm going to need another rope."

"There's one on the canoe. I'll get it."

Will was still lying on his back, unconscious, when Lafleur bound his hands behind a slender tree. He worked quickly and deftly with the rope. As Alison watched, she recalled that Lafleur once told her that rope was the only weapon he brought on his backcountry outings with juvenile delinquents. He would tie them up if they were really bad, which often meant they had tried to kill him or the other counselor.

"These guys were really bad," she said.

"I'm sure," Wallace said. "Good thing you're a great shot."

"It went high," she said. "Too high."

He tried to read her expression and tone but couldn't. They went to the cabin, where Alison spoke gently to Lottie until her eyes fluttered open. They closed again. Wallace looked around for something to use as a backboard so they could transport her without moving her spine, just in case she had neck or disk injuries. Then Lottie moaned and woke. When Alison asked if she could get up, she nodded slightly.

"We have to take you to the hospital," her niece said. "Can you walk at all?"

Alison and Wallace helped her to the skiff. Will was still out of it when they passed him. When they got to the water, George interrupted his whimpering to scream at them.

"I may be back to hang you up and gut you," Lafleur said. "Or I may just leave you here for the coyotes."

They helped Lottie into the skiff. On the trip upriver, Alison held Lottie and Lafleur drove the boat, trying to keep the ride smooth. In Newcomb, he called for an ambulance and then notified the rangers. While they waited, Alison told him what happened at the cabin. She rode with her aunt to the hospital in Saranac Lake. Lafleur stayed behind to wait for a ranger. He locked his pistol in his truck and pocketed the key. He didn't think Will or George had much chance of getting loose, but he warned the first ranger who showed up that there were guns on the property. After a second ranger arrived, the three went downriver in the skiff.

When they arrived at the cabin, Will was still groggy and sluggish. They put him in Lottie's boat and George in the other boat. On the trip back to Newcomb, the rangers tried to get the brothers to talk.

"She shot me with a fucking arrow!" George replied each time he was asked what happened.

Will didn't say anything.

41

Alison woke before dawn and made coffee. She walked to the spot by the maple where she'd buried the dogs and offered a little prayer for them. She went back inside the cabin, cleaned her cup and the coffeepot, and made sure everything would be in order for Lottie's eventual return. Alison had visited her aunt in the hospital the previous morning and spent the rest of the day cleaning the cabin, removing signs of blood, and digging the graves. She also replaced the screen. She didn't do anything about the birdshot embedded in the bedroom walls. She refused to let Wallace help. Now she opened her duffel bag and made sure she had all her clothes and books, including her heavy coat. She loaded the canoe, pushed off, and paddled north. She inhaled the slightly metallic scent of the river and the fragrance of the balsams and cedars. She also detected a strong hint of autumn in the air. She recognized the smell from years past. It was her favorite season.

She stopped paddling and let her hand drift in the cool Hudson. Her river, she thought. As perpetual as the forest, as the mountains. She tried to memorialize this moment, breathing deep, feeling herself completely present. When she paddled again, she felt the strength of her back and shoulders, which she'd gained over the summer. She wondered again, for the hundredth time in the past few days, whether this was where she belonged.

In Newcomb, she called Wallace from the pay phone, and he picked her up about an hour later. He didn't get out of the black truck. She tossed her bag in the bed and climbed in the cab.

"How are you?" he said.

"Good. I'm good."

"Everything went the way you wanted it to down there?"

"Not everything. But on balance it went well."

"Good for you," he said.

"I do want to talk about it," Alison said. "But not until you're done driving. I don't want to distract you."

Lafleur had prepared himself to be supportive. He'd finally let himself think about what Alison was doing and decided against allowing himself any expectations. It wasn't up to him. There was probably not anything he could do to change it. Women choose. It's the way of things. And if he believed that, then anything else was simply unnatural or at least prone to all sorts of disappointments.

Alison tried to gauge exactly how she felt as they headed north on Route 73 toward the B&B. The landscape was still spectacular. She felt a little thrill when they pulled in the dirt drive. She hoped she'd never get over that feeling.

"When is your next trip?"

"Tomorrow."

"Do you have time to talk?"

"For you darlin', of course."

Alison left her bag in the truck. He walked to the upstairs deck, the place from which he surveyed his world, and sat down. She sat a few feet away from him.

"So I have a question," she said.

"Okay."

"How do you feel about New York? I mean the city."

"I've been there. It was interesting."

"But not someplace you'd want to live."

"Don't really know how I could do that and do this," Wallace said, looking around. "Are you inviting me?"

"Not right away. I'd have to get settled there first. But that's premature anyway. I just wanted to know. I was pretty sure you'd say something like that. You're kind of married to the mountains."

"That's one way to look at it," Wallace said, thinking this was going just about the way he'd thought.

"And how are you set for help? Were you still counting on me to work with you with both businesses?"

"I've been thinking that it's possible you might not be here. That I might need to make other arrangements. And I haven't. Though I can," Lafleur said. "If you need to be going, it will be okay."

"Oh, good," Alison said. "Though you say that a little too easily. Like

I'm already gone or something."

"And you're not?"

"Do you want to keep me employed for a little while longer?" she said.

Lafleur stretched, then ran his hands through his hair. He sighed and shook his head. He looked up.

"Or what, am I just another in a series of women who found a place on your payroll and in your bed?" Alison said. "Are you ready for me to go? Get on to the next one? Maybe Susan's ready to come back."

Wallace looked at the mountains. He didn't say anything and let the pause linger there awkwardly.

"If you want to end this, you can," he said. "You don't have to fight your way clear. I'm hoping you won't do that. This has been great. Let's leave it that way."

"That's it?" Alison stood and turned away from him. She felt like crying and wasn't going to. Not here.

"How long were you going to stay? This week? Until Labor Day?"

"I was hoping to stay through December or another year. But you know what? No. Good luck." She started down the stairs, then slowed down. "I'm going to need a ride."

Lafleur followed her down.

"I know," he said. "What did you mean about December?"

Alison shook her head. "What difference does that make?"

"A lot. That way I won't have to hire somebody else." He had that look he used when he said things just to provoke people, which he'd done with her once or twice. It was teasing, more or less.

"I essentially invited you to share my life and you didn't even react. What the hell am I supposed to do with that? That you're so very interested."

He reached down and took her hand. She pulled it away.

"Fact is there are a lot of ways to say goodbye, and it appeared for a while you were trying out some of them until you found the right one." Lafleur stepped back. "If you've got four more months, or a year, then for sure. Spend them here."

"I asked them if I could postpone taking classes until January. But they said I couldn't because there's only one iteration of the classes. And if you miss the fall semester you don't have the foundation for the spring. So I asked them if I could postpone for a year. There's only six students in my cohort this year, and they said there was no way to determine now whether there would be a place next year and that I already had this one. They also couldn't guarantee the assistantship and stipend, which they said I could still get this year. Which I need."

"So you have to go?"

"I was hoping not to. But if I'm going to accept this, I do."

"Then how much time do you have?"

"Three days. Maybe two. I have to find a place to live."

Lafleur reached into the truck bed and grabbed her bag. "There's often a way to work things out," he said.

Alison walked ahead of him to the back of the house and held the door so he could carry the bag inside. As he brushed past, she said, "I'll let you know."

42

When Kirkland phoned in late October, Lafleur was home. He had a buck gutted and hanging out beyond the house. It had taken him a week, but it had been a good week. After finding sign of the buck, Lafleur built a blind and returned each day. On the last morning, he set out before dawn in the pale light of a clear sky and a moon that was nearly full. He was almost disappointed when it was over, though grateful for the single clean shot. The buck fell immediately and was already dead by the time Lafleur walked to where it had emerged from a thick stand of trees.

Alison was up early those mornings as well. She would go first to the window of her tiny apartment on the eighth floor and look out at the skyscrapers of lower Manhattan. She couldn't see the moon but tried to distinguish its light from the artificial glow of the city. In the afternoons and evenings, she sometimes walked a few blocks west from the subway to visit the narrow park along the Hudson, near where it merged with the sea.

"What are you doing now that whitewater season is over?" Kirkland asked Lafleur.

"Just thinking about going to the butcher and exactly what venison I'm going to want for my freezer."

"Is it good?"

"It's very good. I'm thinking about stew. Steaks. Sausages. Ground meat."

"Nice. I'm calling because I thought you'd be interested. The grand jury came back with charges of criminally negligent homicide and obstruction against two of those artists who were in the raft."

"I guess that's nearly the end of it."

"Not quite," Kirkland said. "They both had to spend a night in jail up there because they didn't have their own lawyers, didn't expect to get put in jail, and didn't immediately have anybody to post bail. They finally went home the next day. I was told they could probably plead guilty to misdemeanors since neither one has any kind of criminal record."

"I'm sure they don't want to spend a week up here going through a trial," Lafleur said. "Maybe they'll get probation and community service or something like that. It depends on the D.A. and the judge. I doubt that anybody wants a trial."

"And it's a hike from New York City."

"Not as far as you might think. About three hundred miles."

"How is Alison?"

"The last time I saw her she was good."

"She's not up there anymore?"

"Well, Jack, she's such a fine psychologist that they asked her to come back and finish her Ph.D. That's where she is. To answer your question, I saw her about two weeks ago. There among the deep canyons of New York City. She seemed fine."

"I can't picture you in New York City."

"Guess I'm what you'd call adaptable."

"I also heard from the State Police investigator that you two had an incident at the end of the summer," Kirkland said. "What happened?"

"A couple guys came up and made a little trouble at her aunt's cabin on the river. But it turned out all right."

"What happened?"

"Well, that's still in court. Or heading there. These guys, they were in jail for a while also. This was after they got out of the hospital." Wallace chuckled. "And they've still got some felony assault charges. Alison and her aunt have a court order of protection. I suspect that if they so much as look at either of those women the judge will revoke bail. He was not a happy judge. It seems likely they'll do some prison time, too. But you never know."

"Was Alison hurt?"

"No. I'd say not. Her aunt had her jaw broken in a couple places, but it's healed nicely. She's got her tongue back anyway. The thing was they killed her dogs. But she's got two more now, from the same breeder who trains those shorthairs, two more pointers, and a third one, a bull mastiff, that's supposed to be the pack leader. That one's for security. Her cabin's more like a kennel these days. You approach with the dogs out, you take your chances."

"But you go there."

"About once a week. Alison asked me to keep an eye on her. I should say me and the carpenter. Her aunt has been winterizing the place. Insulation and Sheetrock."

"So you're still seeing her?"

"You know, Jack, that's not up to me. I can tell you, though, that she's planning to come for Thanksgiving. After that it's hard to say."

Before hanging up, Kirkland said he'd stop in sometime. Lafleur said he'd be welcome, though he might be busy around the holidays. It turned out later that he wasn't. Alison phoned the week before Thanksgiving and said she had too much work to get away. What if he came down to the city? Wallace had a hunting group booked in the B&B for the four-day weekend. He was going to guide them that Friday and planned to give her the option of coming along. So he couldn't really leave.

"Then I guess we'll have to postpone," Alison said.

"I don't have much going on until Christmas and just some guests coming then."

"That's going to be difficult for me. It's a crush through the end of the semester. And this is the crucial one. I have to do the work. It's a lot. I can't leave."

"Then you probably wouldn't want a visitor," Wallace said.

"You could come," she replied. "I just wouldn't have much time. But you could."

"Let me see what's possible." He tried to read her enthusiasm and couldn't. He wasn't sure.

They discussed their plans for Thanksgiving. Alison thought she'd drive up to Connecticut to see her mother and her sister's family for the day. Wallace said he'd probably cook for the hunters, unless they wanted to do it themselves, which a lot of hunters did. He didn't have too many fixed plans after that, though the band was thinking about playing out in Lake Placid for a night or two. Alison brought the conversation to an end.

"I've got to get to my job," she said. "And I'm teaching tomorrow, plus there's a meeting. So I have to go."

"Sure. Call me when you've got time. I'd like to hear about everything."

"I will."

Wallace pulled on his heavy boots and parka, poured more coffee, and took the cup and his legal pad outside on his upstairs deck. There was still some warmth in the wind out of the west, though the Great Range was a darker hue than yesterday. The hardwoods were now all leafless, and everything they had dropped was starting to go brown. There was already a little snow up in the High Peaks. He thought he might try to organize a winter rafting trip to Costa Rica or Belize and began taking notes on what he'd need to know or find out and what clients might be up for something like that, how to make the bills and checks balance. He thought maybe Alison could come, if she could find the time.

MICHAEL VIRTANEN is a graduate of Colgate University and the University at Albany, where he earned a master's degree in English. His first novel, *Within a Forest Dark*, was published by Lost Pond Press in 2007 and won the Adirondack Center for Writing's award for best fiction of the year. Virtanen is a veteran journalist whose articles on the Adirondacks have run in newspapers across the country as well as in the magazines *Adirondack Life* and *Adirondack Explorer*. On one assignment, he suffered frostbite on his toes while skiing through the High Peaks Wilderness, but he hasn't lost his zest for adventure in the mountains. He enjoys hiking, paddling, and rock climbing. He lives with his wife, Saundra, in upstate New York.